Gelignite Jack

A SWEET COMEDY

APOSTROPHE

EAST FORTIETH

Gelignite Jack

A Sweet Comedy

Apostrophe

East Fortieth

Paul Davies

Véhicule Press

MONTREAL

Published with the assistance of The Canada Council.

Set in Perpetua by ECW Type & Art, Oakville, Ontario.
Printed by Imprimerie d'Édition Marquis Ltée.

Dépôt légal, Bibliothèque nationale du Québec and
the National Library of Canada, 3rd quarter 1996.

CANADIAN CATALOGUING IN PUBLICATION DATA

Davies, Paul, 1954–

Gelignite Jack

ISBN 1-55065-080-7

1. Title.

PS8557.A8197G44 1996   C813'.54   C96-900494-X
PR9199.3.D29G44 1996

The setting, context, characters, and circumstance
of this story suite are fictional, even as real or
historical places, events, or situations may be described.

Distributed in Canada by General Distribution Services, Don Mills, Ontario,
and in the United States by Login Publishers Consortium, Chicago, Illinois.

Published by Véhicule Press,
P.O.B. 125, Place du Parc Station, Montreal, Quebec H2W 2M9.
Printed in Canada on alkaline paper.

for J. M. D.

I am all at once what Christ is,
        since he was what I am, and
This Jack, joke, poor potsherd, patch,
        matchwood, immortal diamond,
Is immortal diamond.

GERARD MANLEY HOPKINS
"That Nature Is a Heraclitean Fire and
of the Comfort of the Resurrection"

A Sweet Comedy

Though your heart it may be broken
And life about to end
No matter what you've lost, be it a home, a love, a friend
Like the Mary Ellen Carter, rise again.

STAN ROGERS

1

'They were all called "Gelignite Jack," whether their name was Jack or not. It was a little epithet for the *métier*. His real name was Geoff. Geoff Douglas.'

'What did they do, Lindsay?'

'During World War II, civil defence volunteers were taught how to defuse unexploded enemy bombs. You know, the ones that were dropped in the air raids, but didn't go off.'

'I've seen them in pictures, sticking up from the rubble, or just lying in the street! Frightening things. But what does "gelignite" mean?'

'That's the explosive glycerine goop packed inside. They usually had to open the casings and scoop this stuff out to make the bombs safe. It was unstable and volatile, with a powerful ammonia smell that tore at your eyes and nose. Dangerous and unpleasant work, to say the least.'

'So, that's what the one script is about?'

'That, and much more, I think. Each of the three acts deals with different times in his life. I've only read the first several pages carefully.'

Lindsay had picked up the new season scripts from the producer at the Lyceum Theatre, up on Dupont, on the way home from work the day before. Three plays altogether.

'It sounds interesting.'

'Really! Although, when he gave me the scripts, Martin Henry pointed out that women auditioning for *Gelignite Jack* had to be prepared to unbutton their blouse to a brassière top on stage.'

'That's hardly risqué these days,' Andy said.

Like Lindsay, Andy was tall, slender, and attractive, with golden-brown hair. She preferred *Andy* to *Andrea*.

'That's true, but the story does have an eccentric turn. Douglas was killed disarming a bomb in 1945. He was forty-six. It happened in Exeter, in the southwest of England. The explosion had something to do with the timing device. If the bomb wasn't ticking, you could disable it by hammering in this particular rivet that protruded from the casing; if the timer *had* started, however, hitting this striker would detonate it.

'One day, Geoff sat himself on the back of a big bomb, and pounded his hammer down on the pin. Its clock must have started up the *moment* before he swung, because his brilliance was blown to free molecules when it hit.'

'The buttons! What about the buttons?'

'That part was fascinating, although Martin only told me the high points. Geoff had a certain *influence* with things in this world, in a quiet and private way. Like George William Russell, the Irish poet and painter, was said to have.'

'I'm not confused about who Russell is anymore,' Andy said, behind a little wince.

'Oh, sorry,' Lindsay replied with an assuring touch of her hand. 'Anyway, during the last few years of his life, Geoff would help people if they called on him. It had to be at a particular time of day, about eleven o'clock in the morning. He'd see friends and strangers alike — always women — provided they came to the door asking if they could tell him their "story." He would see them in, then they'd sit together on the couch in his study.'

'So, he just sat close to them?'

'Apparently, although Martin said, in real life, it could be quite intimate. Not prurient, mind you. It was an expression of trust, belief, and bonding, if you like. He would lay his head on her chest and listen to her heartbeat — in a kind of trance — while she told him her troubles. Sometimes Geoff would say a few words, some-times not; but afterward, things often *happened* in their lives — or didn't happen, as the case may be.'

'Did he actually cause these things to occur?'

'I can't say, of course. I asked Martin the same thing. He said, if his visitors didn't *truly* think or believe it was genuine, they wouldn't have *been* there. They wouldn't have gone to see him.'

'Can *you* see him?'

'I haven't tried, Andy.'

The two friends shared a confidence. If Lindsay sat quietly and formed an image in her mind — of people, or places — she could sometimes *see* them, as though she were there.

'I suppose Gelignite Geoff was secretive for the same reason you are.'

'Well, if his story is true, my talent pales in comparison.'

'I think they're just different.'

'Maybe — but I hope you know I don't *want* to be secretive. You can't talk about it because it comes and goes. If you tell someone, and then can't crank up a performance on demand, you're a fraud.'

Lindsay rested her head on the palm of her hand. 'We really shouldn't even be talking about it.'

'It's just between us, don't worry.'

Andy glanced at her watch, and her thoughts turned to practical matters. 'Where does the day go? Listen, I'd better get over to Becker's for some bread and stuff. See you in a few minutes.'

'Okay, though you know . . .' Lindsay waited for Andy to stop and look at her. 'We should be trying harder than toast and macaroni all the time! We've grown a little lazy about feeding ourselves.'

'Yes, I know that's true. I'll see what I can find. Bye!'

When Lindsay heard her friend close the outside door behind her, she wondered if she *could* see Geoff Douglas. She sat at the desk in her room and folded her hands on its broad smooth top.

She'd passed through Exeter two years before, during her trip to England. She remembered its great cathedral in particular, although she had not gone inside. The townspeople waited 1,050 years for construction to start, the bus driver had jokingly informed them, from the town's founding in 60 A.D. The church took a further 250 years to build, he'd said, from 1110 to 1360. Then, in May 1942, one chapel, the muniment room above it, three bays of the aisle, and two flying buttresses were destroyed in a split second — something of a miraculous escape, given most of the city was reduced to rubble in heavy bombardment.

Lindsay focussed on the cathedral, and made her memory of it vivid in her mind. She recalled its broad central mass of chiselled stone, its tall spires, towers, large arched windows, its buttresses, and the wall adjacent to the main entrance on the west side, stacked three high with intricate carvings of apostles, evangelists, and unknown sages and martyrs.

She could see the shops and houses along the Cathedral Close — some timbered Tudor, others more modern Georgian and Victorian — as she walked across the lawn around the church beside the large Norman tower on the north side, catching a glimpse of the Tudor portico of Guildhall off to the northwest, aware of the not-too-distant bustle of cars and motorcycles.

Through the arched wooden doors, a small chapel to her right, Lindsay entered the nave, overwhelmed by its size and grandeur. Huge. Magnificent. Massive shafted columns yielding to tremendous stretches of Gothic stone vaulting overhead, the tierceron ribs finished with dozens of colourful carved bosses.

The seating in the nave faced a great screen at the transept. The quire past the screen had fixed seats facing inward, all of beautifully carved wood, with the traditional lamp at each position. She could see an elaborate throne past the quire, the High Altar at the far end, and a spacious chapel beyond it, one of many smaller side chapels. Atop the great screen was the largest organ case Lindsay had ever seen, banks upon banks of polished silver-grey pipes gleaming in the morning sun, which poured through the spokes of the stained glass complex that filled the east wall ahead of her.

The air was radiant with the voices of choristers.

About twenty men and boys, selected for the quality and type of their respective voices, she thought, no doubt singing today in rehearsal. The church was otherwise empty.

Lindsay, not expecting to be noticed, walked to the screen — but she no sooner caught the conductor's glance than she knew she'd been discovered.

He eased her worry by smiling warmly and, with a motion of his hand, invited her to be seated. Even across the breadth of the transept Lindsay was struck by his eyes. She found herself feeling apprehensive — wondering who and what might dwell behind them. Then it occurred to her. 'Of course, *that* is Geoff Douglas! The second act is about his life as a choral conductor.'

The sacred anthem was lengthy — bookended by opening tenor and closing treble solos — with the choral parts in the middle slowly building to a stirring crescendo.

Lindsay had a great affection for choral music. Her knowledge of music in general was competent, though not profound. She'd enjoyed private study during elementary school, but in adolescence had increasingly felt drawn to drama.

When the song concluded, Geoff asked the choristers to rest for a few minutes. He walked over to Lindsay and sat down on the chair beside her.

'That's a particular favourite of mine, "Behold, a white cloud," written in 1907 by Healey Willan while he was still in England and studying with Vaughan Williams. He's gone to live in Canada now. Regrettably, we only perform it at the harvest service. I have to have a boy sing the soprano part, of course.'

'It was lovely.'

'I'm always glad when people come in to listen,' Geoff replied, 'although I'm afraid we don't get many. Are you visiting? You don't sound like a native.'

'Yes, I'm visiting — from Canada, as it happens.'

Lindsay found herself a little tongue-tied.

'Perhaps I might come to visit you — at your home — in the morning? One day.'

She wasn't sure what had moved her to ask.

Geoff looked into her eyes, and said nothing. Lindsay was neither warmed nor anxious inside, despite his penetrating gaze.

She detected the wisp of a nod.

'What is your name?'

'Lindsay.'

'I'm glad to know you, Lindsay.'

'What can you see, looking at me?' She asked the question lightly, hoping Geoff might respond with some greater wisdom than it petitioned.

'What do I see? Let me think.'

He looked into her eyes again, softly. Lindsay felt completely transparent.

'You are young, of great intelligence. And well educated.'

He thought for a moment.

'You are also impatient to learn, and regard others with more experience as having something to teach you. You are eager to draw them out.'

Lindsay was worried suddenly. Did he mean she might tend to abuse situations? Was she doing so now?

'Approached with your sincerity and humility, most people would undoubtedly respond kindly and well,' he smiled, precisely discerning the distress in her face. 'An active talented mind such as yours requires a lengthy period of self-discovery and experimentation, something you're undergoing right now. Although awkward at times, it is healthy and necessary. But take note, Lindsay,' he confided, sitting back in the pew, then paused and added, 'I couldn't say this to anyone who might ask how I've come to know it.'

'I understand,' Lindsay returned.

'I believe you have a tragedy to reconcile ahead, or some form of significant sacrifice to make. . .'

A hint of a blush coloured Geoff's face.

'. . . but, you know, you would probably have more astute counsel from the personals column in the Sunday newspaper.'

'I don't think so, Geoff. I will be watchful. Thank you.'

'I'm glad you came to listen today. Goodbye.'

He stood and walked back to his place in front of the choir.

As the voices were raised in song, the sound filled her with joy. She recognized the anthem as Charles Wood's 'Hail, gladdening light.' Again, one great man learning from another, she mused. Vaughan Williams had been Wood's pupil.

Lindsay sat watching Geoff conduct the choir — the brisk concentrated movements of his hands, arms, and face — understanding why he'd suddenly discounted his advice, and why (according to the playwright) he usually said so little. It was often hard, she thought, to distinguish between mystical knowledge, observation, and intuition.

'I must go now,' she muttered.

As she passed back through the west door, she could see the roof tiles of the house opposite through the window in her room, above her folded hands.

Andy had returned. She knew Lindsay never wanted to talk about what she'd seen, right afterward. As it was, she would have found her friend particularly disinclined that moment. Uneasy. Usually, she only *saw*. Never before had she been *seen*.

2

Lindsay came across the narrow hallway to Andy's room and sat on the loveseat beside the door, tucking legs and feet among the cushions.

'Andy? I'm feeling discouraged about this auditioning. There must have been fifty others at the Lyceum, all picking up the season.'

'I'm going in with the *belief* they want me. Pick *me*, I say to myself, *I'm* the one you want.'

Lindsay slapped at a sofa pillow, knocking it to the floor.

'That's fine for you,' Lindsay sighed. 'After all, you're talented, fit — and beautiful. You almost glow in the dark! They *want* to pick you the moment you walk into the theatre.'

'Lindsay, I understand if you're feeling unhappy about things today, but you mustn't project that onto me. It can so easily turn into something between us, when we're both just struggling in the same situation.'

Lindsay picked up the cushion.

'Andy, I'm sorry. That was childish of me.'

'When we decided to room together, I thought there might be some tense moments. For instance, if one of us got a part and the other didn't. When we've each had a few jobs, it won't be like one of us has something the other hasn't. You know what I mean? You're working now, I'm working then, and, another time, we're both working. Maybe working the same show! Lindsay! Wouldn't that be fun?'

'That would be *great* fun. Truly.'

'So, I was only trying to pick you up, telling you what goes through my mind. Two heads are usually better than one, when it comes to keeping spirits up.'

'Of course, Andy, you're right. And I appreciate it. It's funny. We have the same experience as other actors and performers. We *can* compete. But, the audition is a whole other thing. Like a separate skill.'

'Sure it is. Some people *only* audition well, while others — a lot of them good — always seem to goof it up. Anyway, somehow, the casting directors know. The right people usually do get the jobs.'

'Funny how that works.'

'Let's ensure it works for us! After all, this whole thing was a leap of faith when we took it on. Imagine us seeing theatre as a *career* choice! You always think it's something others do better. Or, that others have more courage.'

'Not to mention our friends and families saying it's suspect to start with. Unstable, uncertain, competitive. All that.'

'You have to be fueled by a passion for it! Like the rubby in the Dominion the other day.'

'What rubby?' Lindsay asked.

'I was over picking up a few things. When I got to the cash, in comes this guy. He wasn't horribly dirty or anything, but definitely camping in the street. Well, he ambled along between the check-out stands and the windows — then it dawned on him a crowd of people were staring from behind the row of cash registers. His face lit up and, arms outstretched, he burst into song! *Home, home on the range, where the deer and the antelope play!* A big baritone voice — I was convinced he was a failed Broadway star, the way he came alive for his audience there. He sure could sing! In fact, the security guard let him finish, seeing that everyone was enjoying the performance. When he was done, we all applauded! He took a few deep bows and left. It was amazing.'

'Oh, no! That worries me,' fretted Lindsay. 'Are *we* going to end up singing for nickels on street corners?'

'I don't think so. Besides, what it meant to me was how we're *called* to this thing, whatever happens. That bum had found his livery, even if his life is otherwise down-and-out.'

'What do you mean?'

'Sorry to be obscure. It's from Hazlitt, something in one of his essays. Just a sec, I'll read it to you. I marked the spot in the book.'

Andy pulled a paperback down from her bookshelf.

'Here it is: "Actors are the only honest hypocrites. Their life is a voluntary dream; and the height of their ambition is to be beside themselves. They wear the livery of other men's fortunes: their very thoughts are not their own." He's saying the substance of our being is the scripts we bring to life.'

'No plot to our own dramas, then?'

'Only in a manner of speaking,' Andy said with a big smile, 'but never mind. Hazlitt was an old grouch!'

As she got up to leave, Lindsay surveyed the flat. They'd rented adjacent rooms with shared bath on the third floor of a well maintained rooming-house on Bedford Road. Originally an unfinished attic, the ceilings sloped up sharply from the base of the windows, following the roofline.

Lindsay had selected the north-facing room, with the barren vista through its one small window, because it had the large antique desk. She hadn't been optimistic when they'd embarked on their search, but felt comforted when she saw that desk. The modest furnishings in the room across the hall — which was also vacant — had suited Andy nicely, and the rates were reasonable, so they moved in that same afternoon.

The house, on a corner lot, had an unobstructed view to the south from Andy's room — an agreeable tableau of windows, rooftops, apartments, and trees down the way to Varsity Stadium. Now, after a few months there, it was the familiar surrounds of home.

Their landlord, the owner, occupied the first floor with his friend. He drove an old Sunbeam Tiger, which he kept parked at the back. Lindsay loved the car, still in excellent condition despite the abuse of ten years on Toronto streets.

Lindsay's affection for the Sunbeam was, more generally, something she acquired from her father, a British sports car enthusiast. She often joked with her friends that she'd grown up in a vintage auto garage.

'I'd better get off to work, Andy.'

'Okay. See you later.'

Andy, living on her savings, used the time she had during the day to sharpen her acting skills, attending voice and dance classes and the like. She had another three or four months before her financial fuse burned down.

Lindsay was several hundred dollars less fortunate, and worked days at the University of Toronto in the main Sigmund Samuel Library. A huge new library was under construction, but wouldn't be finished for some time yet. Sigmund Samuel was something of a refuge for aspiring artists, writers, actors, and photographers, keeping themselves fed and clothed while they discovered whether or not their hopes and dreams might become ambitions.

Neither Lindsay nor Andy had made many friends since moving to Toronto. Lindsay, the more outgoing of the pair, had several good acquaintances at the library, with whom they socialized from time to time. Andy, more bashful, tended to keep to herself at her classes. Both were raised in Alberta towns, and had met while attending the arts college in Calgary. The previous June, after completing the drama program, they'd promptly packed their bags for Toronto.

Lindsay collected her things, skipped down the back stairs, and out the rear door. The front entrance was used exclusively by the landlord and his friend. The back, used by the roomers, exited alongside the house onto Lowther Avenue. The red sportscar was parked next to the gate in the back garden.

The morning, brilliant and warm for late September, reminded Lindsay it was glorious to be alive. She enjoyed the fall season best of all the year. Still sunny — not too humid — with the attractive colours of the changing leaves. She made her way to Bloor Street and headed for Philosophers' Walk, a narrow grassy pathway situated between the immense west wall of the Royal Ontario Museum and the Royal Conservatory of Music.

She'd been working at the library for three months, and had settled into a pleasant routine. Pleasant except for an undercurrent of dissatisfaction among her co-workers. Like the episode in *Alice in Wonderland*, she often thought, when someone protests that they aren't crazy, and someone else replies that, if they *weren't* crazy, they wouldn't *be* there. For anyone with talent or ambition, being there — having to work there — was a nagging humilation.

Today, as she walked along, Lindsay smiled inwardly, noting the similarity between her touchstone from *Alice* and what Martin had said about the belief of Gelignite Geoff Douglas's visitors. If they didn't believe, they wouldn't have been there.

Crossing Hoskin Avenue, the stone clock tower a short way ahead down the backside breadth of Hart House, Lindsay spotted a superb Morgan roadster — a 1949 model, two-tone, with leather bonnet straps.

'Daddy always said he wanted one of the Morgan three-wheelers, the one with the big J.A.P. v-twin in front,' Lindsay said to the Hart House car-park attendant, who happened to be standing beside her. He exposed a row of broken teeth, punctuated here and there with steel caps.

A smile, she thought.

3

Late the following Saturday morning, Lindsay and Andy were riding the subway up from King Street in silence. They were alone in the car, bright with fluorescent lighting and advertising posters. Both stared absently through the window, watching the vague shapes of pillars, beams, and signal lanterns pass by in the darkness of the tunnel.

Andy spoke first.

'That really didn't go very well.'

'I bet you were wonderful! *I* was the one who flubbed it,' Lindsay corrected her friend.

The Royal Alexandra Theatre Company had called in response to their résumés the day before, inviting them to audition for a new musical. The plays coming up at the Lyceum had more appeal for Lindsay, but she felt she had better try out for everything that she could.

'I think I lost my nerve when we couldn't find the street entrance. The building next to the theatre is so drab. You wouldn't think it was part of the Royal Alex.'

'It's not part of the theatre, really. It's mostly offices and stuff. The top floor was taken over for studios a while back, as the theatre operation grew.'

'I went into the hall, where normally there might be fifty people dancing and singing, to find there was only *The Table* at the end. Empty but for the five producers sitting there, looking like they'd seen about ten too many girls for one day.'

'That's right,' Lindsay laughed. 'I could have mistaken them for mediaeval inquisitors!'

'What did you do?'

'For the dance number? I did that bit from *West Side Story*. What else! My song was "Somebody Loves Me." I think that went over pretty well, but they really are looking for dancers for this.'

Andy drew a long breath before continuing. 'I sure wish we came away from these things feeling more satisfied.'

'Me, too. But, don't forget that thing about competent people not auditioning well. I think it was pretty good we got called up in the first place. They probably had a thousand résumés.'

'That's true. Anyway, we don't have to wait long. They said they'd let us know on Monday.'

'Are you going to stay home to get the phone?'

Their rooming-house had a payphone installed in a nook on the second floor.

'Yes, though I think Victor's home on Monday. He's a saint about taking messages.'

'Speaking of saints, Lindsay, did you read any more of the *Gelignite Jack* play?'

'I finished it. It's very touching. I also read the second, and scanned through the third.'

'What are the other two about?'

'One's about a scientist and this important experiment he under-takes, but gets fooled about its outcome. The other's about a motor-cycle racer — well, more about the *engineering* of his motorcycle — for a speed record in the 1930s. An interesting story. It really captures the sense of *beauty* they saw in their work.'

'Seems to be an historical theme at the Lyceum this year.'

'Martin Henry said that's what they intend. They'll be promoting the season as three historical dramas.'

'Here's our stop,' Andy said as they rose from their seats. The train doors slid open to reveal the green ceramic walls of St. George Station facing them across the platform. 'Why don't we go down to Queen's Park and walk off some of this strain?'

'Good idea.'

Approaching the park, strolling in the sunshine, Lindsay felt more relaxed.

'I don't think I told you, but I had the most beautiful thing happen here one Sunday on my way to work. It was a misty morning — a proper fog, really. I couldn't see any distance ahead, and there were hardly any cars about. Well, all of a sudden I hear the sound of bagpipes drifting through the mist. It was all the more beautiful for being so unlikely.'

'You never know what to expect around here,' Andy replied.

Their rooming-house was in the Annex, the downtown neighbour-hood north of the University of Toronto, from Bloor Street up to the old CNR tracks, so-named because the land was annexed by the City of Toronto in the 1880s. The large stone houses that typically lined the streets had long before been divided into flats or rooms, largely to service the successive fleets of young people attending the school. The old homes were little less handsome for it, their gardens well-populated with stately mature trees. A charming area, Lindsay thought, except for a few clumps of ugly apartment build-ings congregated along stretches of road the City had seen fit to modernize after the war.

On the eastern edge of the Annex was Yorkville, notorious of late as a gathering zone for hippies and other transients and bums. Lindsay and Andy avoided the stretch altogether, except for the bookstore on the corner where Yorkville ended at Avenue Road. A short walk west of there, on the south side of Bloor, was Rochdale College, an apartment tower built with public funds, completed a few years before and opened as a free school.

Lindsay often recalled her father's understanding of Yorkville and Rochdale, as improbable social adventures resulting from the 'new' generation, the tremendous wave of children appearing after the war, suddenly coming to adulthood — with ideas.

Lindsay had gone over to Rochdale a few weeks back, but had been stopped at the door. Apart from the education project failing rapidly and spectacularly, the building's remains had become something of an armed camp, a few tenacious hold-outs making a tense last stand against their own eviction.

She finally gained access, telling one of the bullies in the entrance-way that she wanted to buy a doctorate. Strictly speaking, academic qualifications were not recognized at Rochdale College. Degrees were granted exclusively on a cash basis.

This cash being important to the residents' cause, Lindsay was promptly escorted to the stationery office where she put down the last $100 from her savings for a certificate. Doctor of Philology. People often bought humorous credentials — Bachelor of Bullshit, Doctor of Doughnuts, Master of Melancholy — but Lindsay wanted hers to be a degree in Philology.

Every once in a while Andy called her 'Doctor,' or 'Doc.'

'I like that, Doc. That comic fringe. It's not always so humorous, of course. Remember the man who fell out of the window at Rochdale, right onto the sidewalk at Karen's feet?' Karen, a mutual friend, worked in a café a few doors down from the Lyceum.

'That was horrible,' she continued, 'but, what about the night I was passing by here and some engineering students blew *Charge of*

23

the Light Brigade on their cornets?! I laughed, imagining the old Vets on the park benches leaping to attention in a sleepy stupor!'

'I wish, for them, it *was* only a sleepy stupor, Andy.'

'I wonder what they do in winter? I guess there's shelters and stuff.'

Lindsay returned them to lighter themes.

'One night last summer, Brian — my friend at the library — was walking along the Danforth when he saw a priest sitting in a restaurant window with a sleazy girl. Have I told you this story?'

'No, I don't think so — what happened?'

'Well, he stopped for a closer look, and this priest gave him the finger! With a threatening sneer!'

'What!'

'Yes, Brian was stunned! Then, he noticed the whole place was *full* of priests with girls in tight mini-skirts and fishnet stockings!'

Andy's face was bright with amusement.

'Well, *then* he noticed the poster: Priest and Prostitute Night. A masquerade the restaurant hosts from time to time, giving prizes for the best costumes and whatnot.'

They both laughed and laughed, rolling over on the grass, before collapsing quietly in the warm sun.

Lindsay blocked out the clear blue sky with closed eyes. In the brightness under her eyelids she saw the glow of the sun on the cathedral floor. She had been anxious to see it again. To see Geoff.

From where she was seated, at the fountain, she could see the Minstrel's Gallery on the north wall overhead, although she could not make out any of the instruments carved into the angel's hands on the front. Ahead, towering above the screen, were the beautiful round clusters of organ pipes. Lindsay had never been particularly fond of organ music. It was nice, of course — especially in this setting — but she would just as soon hear a choir *a cappella*.

She gazed around the vastness of the empty church, admiring the woodwork, the fine stone carving, dust shimmering in the shafts of light from the huge windows. Although happy to be there, she felt slightly foolish, having arrived to find no one about. A lot of time and effort can be spent trying to bump into someone, she reflected.

Lindsay heard one of the front doors groan, and was thrilled for a moment that it might be Geoff. She believed her vision directed her in productive ways, even though she was not aware of its means.

It was not Geoff. It was a woman. She gave Lindsay a little wave as she approached the fountain. She is *beautiful*, Lindsay thought. Stunning. Wearing a simple cotton blouse and a pleated skirt, both nicely tailored to accent her attractive shape, she had an unself-conscious elegance about her.

Lindsay wondered for a second if the harvest Goddess had taken form in common dress.

'I am looking for the Choirmaster,' she announced courteously. Lindsay sensed it was the friendly tone of someone who had enjoyed few friends in her life. Too beautiful to allow others, even other women, to feel completely comfortable in her company. And who knows what other talents to further isolate her from others less gifted, who could not comprehend her joys and sorrows.

Lindsay felt a swell of love in her heart for this person, aware at the same time she was a stranger, and that she had drawn out this feeling on the strength of a glance.

'I don't think there's anyone here. I was hoping to see him, too.'

'My name is Erin. How do you do.'

'I'm Lindsay. How do you do.'

'Are you a friend of Geoff's?'

'No, no, I'm not. I only met him here in the church for the first time . . . just . . . the other day. At a rehearsal.'

'Do you live here in Exeter? What brought you to the cathedral to hear the choir?'

'No, I don't live in England; I'm on a visit. The truth is, I just found myself outside the church and came in. I love choral music.'

'Do you sing?'

'Not really. Well, yes — but not like that. I sing show tunes. I've been studying singing and dancing — and acting — for popular theatre.'

'That's lovely, Lindsay. I'm sure you will do well.'

'I haven't actually gotten a proper role, yet. Only unpaid spots.'

'You are just getting started! That is how you work up to larger roles — and paying roles — and a career. It takes time. The difficulty, of course, is keeping up your enthusiasm, and keeping body and soul together while you do!'

'Are you an actress, Erin? You certainly could be. You're beautiful, and you have a lovely voice.'

'Thank you! That's kind of you to say. I am a singer.'

'I should have guessed. Are you here to sing for Geoff?'

'No, I just wanted to speak with him.'

The light went out of Erin's eyes as she spoke.

'Did I say something wrong?'

'No, I'm sorry. It's complicated. A rift between what is possible, in practical terms, and what might be desired for our friendship.'

Lindsay could see she had accidentally directed their conversation to uneasy ground, and attempted to recover.

'Tell me about singing, Erin. Are you a professional?'

'Yes, I am. If you lived in England, you would probably know my name, having an interest in voice.'

Lindsay felt a jolt run through her. Erin! Of course! Erin *Powell*!

'I *do* know your name! You're Erin Powell, the great mezzo! I'm so sorry, I didn't make the connexion at first.'

Erin laughed warmly, her eyes sparkling. 'That is very sweet. Never mind. I'm flattered you know me at all.'

'Personally, I don't think there's any performance more demanding than recital singing. It's ironic, isn't it? You *need* an informed audience and they need you; but an informed audience demands so *much* of you.'

'They also return as much,' said Erin. 'For a performer, there is no greater reward.'

'But it must be unnerving, as well as sublime.'

'Well, I want people to love me. That's why I'm out there. I want people to hear something beautiful that will fill them with good emotions. And, on a personal level, I want to do my best so that I can love myself. I want to leave feeling proud of who I am, knowing I have honoured the tradition.'

'Still, I'd find it quite scary,' Lindsay replied. Geoff's comment suddenly echoed through her mind. She worried that she might be taking unkind advantage of a famous performer. 'Do you mind my asking you these things? I'm just beginning my career, and am eager to know what you experience, and how you get along.'

'No, I don't mind at all. And, yes, I *am* nervous on stage. Always. A lot of that is put to rest with preparation, and a thorough prior knowledge of the technical aspects; as well, while I'm singing, I talk to myself.'

She hesitated, almost imperceptibly. 'Are you interested in this? It doesn't have much to do with theatre, really.'

'In a way it does — and, yes, I am interested. When I watch a recital, I often stare at the singer's face, wondering what's going on behind their eyes.'

'Mostly, I think about colour — about how I'm going to colour each word, what each word means, how I can best communicate each; also, I consider what I want to say with each word, syllable, and note, and what tone I can apply to emphasize the meaning of each word — various aspects of colour and phrasing.'

Lindsay began to feel she had been away too long; but, she was reluctant to leave, reluctant to disrupt the conversation.

'Plus, you are *performing*. You want to look good and all of that.'

'Well, I certainly try to! I hope my makeup is okay, that I've got no lipstick on my teeth. And I hope none of my spit lands on people in the first row!'

They laughed conspiratorially, holding hands.

'And I hope my face doesn't look ugly when I have difficult vowels to shape,' Erin added.

Lindsay laughed again, bent forward on the pew. A tear rolled down her cheek before she composed herself.

'I can't imagine how much you have to consider, moment by moment — so much more than acting in a drama — weighing all of those different vital qualities, note by note.'

'I think time — "real" time, I mean — expands with all the thoughts I have, with all the subtexts.'

'That's part of the gift, isn't it? I don't think anyone who isn't born with these essentials can be taught to sing. The raw material must be inborn.'

Lindsay knew she had to be getting back. The feeling grew ever more urgent as the seconds ticked past.

'There's so much more I would like to ask you, but I think I'd better be going. Seeing you, talking with you, has been *enriching*, Erin.'

'Thank you, Lindsay. I had best be going, too. I will stop in for Geoff another time. Goodbye.'

As she passed the vestibule, Lindsay could see the sunlit bark of a large oak tree in Queen's Park.

Andy was holding her hand.

Lindsay was shocked to see they were not alone.

'Can you see them, Andy?' she whispered.

'No, of course I can't. What do you mean?'

'This isn't something *seen*. They are *here*.'

'Who?' Andy said, trying hard to comprehend.

Lindsay stared at them, awestruck. The words came to her lips unconsciously, involuntarily.

Hail Raphael, Spirit of Healing,

Hail, Ariel, Strength of GOD, and Uriel, His Light.

She trembled with apprehension.

'Is this about what Geoff told me?' asked Lindsay, feeling ridiculous for saying something so trivial.

The answer came, however, from Milton. A verse from Milton, surfacing in her thoughts.

> . . . *[A] grateful mind*
> *By owing, owes not, but still pays, at once*
> *Indebted and discharged.*

Lindsay, visibly upset, did not understand.

'I'm sorry, I don't know what that means!'

> *That which before us lies in daily life,*
> *Is the prime Wisdom.*

'What?' Andy cried, 'I don't see anything.'

'It's okay, Andy,' Lindsay replied, confused and depressed, 'it's okay. It must have been my imagination running away with me.'

Sitting alone together on the grass, Lindsay squeezed her friend's hand warmly.

4

Lindsay sat down in the coffee room at the library. Monday, mid-morning. Coffee break. Andy was at home, waiting patiently for the Royal Alex to call.

'Sure, *very* funny, if I don't shrivel from radiation poisoning!'

'What was that, Brian?' Lindsay had walked in at the end of a story he was telling the others seated there with him.

'A birthday present a friend of mine made for me. We're both Bob Dylan fans — do you like Bob Dylan?'

'Yes, I do. Though we don't have a record player at home yet, so we can only listen to what they play on the radio.'

'Well, there's this one, somewhat intense, ballad of his — Dylan invented a new language for popular music, you know, with his surreal poetry and lyrics. Well, this one's about the corruption of American thinking because of consumerism. *Money doesn't talk it swears, obscenity that really cares*, and so on. In one verse, where he's talking about the profanity of commercialization, he sings, "Flesh-coloured Christs that glow in the dark." So, my friend went down to the Catholic store on Dundas and bought a big plastic crucifix with a figure of Jesus attached. Then, up to the Toronto Watch Hospital for a bottle of radium paint, which they use to illuminate the tiny dots on watch hands and faces. Four coats of this paint and — *voilà!* — one murky white, if not flesh-coloured, Christ glowing in the dark. I put it up in the corridor at home. Still gives me a start when I see it sometimes!'

Lindsay grinned amiably as Kathleen, Harvey, and Monty laughed at the story a second time.

'He must be a master of improvisation,' she said.

'He might be, if he could knit his personality together better. I don't mean he has any major psychological problems, really. He's just a little too bright for his own good. Ends up running around wired half the time with a dozen or more things on the go.'

'How's the Try-Out Trail, Lindsay?' Kathleen asked.

'A little discouraging, I'm afraid. Andy and I went down to the Royal Alex on Saturday for an audition, but I'm not hopeful for myself. It's a glitzy musical. Andy's more suited to that sort of thing. I stand a better chance at the Lyceum. I picked up the season last week.'

'So, what do they have on offer?'

'Three historical plays. The first will be mounted by November; the second in January; the last, next March.'

'What are they about?'

'One is the story of a choral conductor and mystic in the '30s and '40s who gets killed in the war. Another's about building a speed record motorcycle. The third is about a scientist.'

'Which scientist?' Harvey asked.

Harvey was unique among the young people working at Sigmund Samuel. He had realized his ambition already, finishing a graduate degree in pure mathematics. He didn't have the knack for teaching, however, and he didn't know initially that pure math has no relevance to the material world; but, he loved it and went right through the master's program before running out of steam.

'The name is Michelson. The story has to do with an experiment of his that went wrong.'

'It wasn't that the experiment went wrong,' Harvey gently corrected, 'in fact, it was critical to the advancement of physics. With that one crucial result, Michelson paved the way for the Theory of Relativity.'

'Why is his career counted a failure then?'

'It can't really be counted a *failure*, though I understand why someone would say that — and why it would be great material for a play. Here's the basic story: Albert Michelson's passion was the accurate measurement of the speed of light. He began working on the problem in the late 1870s when he was a science instructor at the U.S. Naval Academy. He went to study optics in Europe, then he returned to the United States to teach at Case in Cleveland. Within four years or so, he'd come up with an excellent value — which stood for quite a long time, until he bettered it himself.'

'So, the great experiment was about the speed of light?'

'In part, yes, but it had more to do with what was out in outer space. Scientists and philosophers had debated the question for centuries: Did the earth travel through an empty void, or was space full of "stuff"? The popular belief was that the earth moved through some kind of motionless stuff, called the "ether." Michelson built an instrument to determine the truth.'

'Is this going to get technical? I'm interested to know, but coffee time is not infinite!' Lindsay smiled brightly.

'It's somewhat technical, but I'll try to make a simple explanation. Besides, if you're going to try out for the play, you should probably know. It will give you a better grasp of the various characters' missions. The device he invented was called an "interferometer." What it did was break a light beam in two, send the parts along different paths for a stretch, and then rejoin them. If the speed or distance travelled by one part was different from the other, they would rejoin out of phase and form a banded interference pattern.'

'I'm with you so far,' Lindsay said.

Harvey was interrupted as Jim, who worked down in the stacks, pulled up a chair with one hand to join the others at the table. Propped between the thumb and third finger of the other he held a paper cup full of fresh coffee.

'What's Harvey on about?'

'He's telling me about an American scientist at the turn of the century who worked in optics,' Lindsay explained.

'Now,' Monty piped up, 'this is something that interests me! In fact, you know, I was gazing out the window, lying in bed with Betty this morning . . .'

Suddenly Jim laughed uproariously, eclipsing Monty's comment. Huge and heartfelt laughter. He didn't fancy Monty's girlfriend Betty, finding her distastefully skinny and irritating in conversation.

'Does my lying in bed with Betty give you *impure* thoughts, Jim?'

Jim blanched. Expressionless, he stood, tossed his unopened cup in the trash, and walked out of the room.

The table was silent for a moment. Then Lindsay and Brian began to laugh, at which Monty nervously rubbed his palms together. Kathleen found it all very awkward. She tried to ease the situation by encouraging Harvey to carry on with his story.

'Sure, Kathleen,' he complied. 'Where was I? Oh, yes. Over the years Michelson — with his colleague Edward Morley, a chemist — refined the interferometer. They built one that split a beam of light and sent the parts at ninety degrees to each other before rejoining them. With this arrangement, they could test for the ether.'

'How's that?' Lindsay asked.

'If the earth does move through an ether, it will affect the light; everything otherwise equal, light moving with the earth should cover more ground than the part bent across its path at ninety degrees, which would be impeded by the ether. An interference pattern would form when the parts were rejoined.'

'And did it?'

'No. No difference. They conducted the experiment several times over a number of years — lastly in 1887, with a very sophisticated setup. No fringes. No ether. They failed.'

'But, as you said before, it wasn't *really* a failure. Michelson only "failed" because he set out to prove that there *was* an ether. If they had set out to prove that there was *no* ether, then the experiment would have been a "success"!'

'Exactly. I marvelled at that irony when I was studying the stuff. Strangely, though, the scientific establishment hasn't seen it that way, by and large. It didn't help that Michelson continued to insist that there *was* an ether to the end of his life.'

'That conviction is hard to imagine now,' Lindsay said.

'It remains,' Harvey added, 'that this experiment stood the whole of theoretical physics on its head. The grand slam came in 1905, when Einstein announced his Special Theory of Relativity. A new physical description for the universe.'

'And what happened to Michelson?' Lindsay asked.

'He got the Nobel Prize in 1907 for his work in optics. While it was early in the history of the prize, he was the first American to win for science. Although, he never accepted Relativity.'

'And this *belief* is what describes him — or his experiment, at least — as a failure! That's fascinating. Thanks, Harvey.'

'You *are* welcome. Math and physics are not big party favourites, you know? I can hardly remember the last time I had somebody interested enough to listen like that.'

'You do yourself an unkindness,' Brian volunteered. 'Hearing yarns like this is one of the nice things about working here.'

'That's right, Harvey,' Kathleen said, 'that was interesting. It's nice some people have had that focus, anyway.'

'Sure it is,' Harvey agreed. 'But it's easy to make it sound like that when you're summing up a lifetime in a few sentences. Really, these guys were just getting up morning after morning, probably spending most of their lives in a dreamy and disconnected world of their own.'

'I often feel my life is dreamy and disconnected,' Lindsay confessed. 'I don't *mind* that; but, I don't feel like a passenger ticketed for a specific destination, rolling down the rails of life. Instead, for me the presentiment is more like I'm touring an art gallery, taking in the paintings — discrete episodes in some bigger panorama.'

'I think the ticketed stuff emerges slowly as you grow older,' Harvey acknowledged. 'Mainly, I think, because you're less content; that is, you want more comforts, more stability, and more money. Don't you think those things come at the cost of that reflective episodic life?'

'You should at least be dating,' Kathleen opined. She was not comfortable alone and had difficulty imagining someone not dating.

'Dating?!' Lindsay blurted. 'I don't have time for that right now, Kathleen. Getting involved with a person takes up a *lot* of energy. I will, don't worry! After I've gained some ground in theatre.'

'Or, when the right man sweeps you off your feet,' Harvey added.

'I suppose that's possible.'

'You went out with Jim Matthews, didn't you?' Kathleen asked.

'Yes — what a disaster! We went to see *Marat/Sade* at Cinema Lumière. A brilliant film. I wished I'd seen the original on Broadway. Do you know the story? Marat was a fragile socialist visionary at the time of the French Revolution. His belief, expressed in the play, is that if a person has a loaf of bread, he should break it in two and share it with his neighbour. De Sade makes the more intuitively compelling argument that people are motivated by the needs of their own survival, that they will not allot what bread they have at the expense of their own welfare. Anyway, we got out of the theatre, and

34

Jim — ever the naïve optimist — said, "I don't know how *anyone* could have sympathized with de Sade." Then yours truly — the social pragmatist — returns, "Oh, *I* don't know how anyone could have sympathized with *Marat*." The sidewalk split to a cavernous gulf between us — figuratively, of course — and that was it.'

Lindsay sighed. Her friends smiled sympathetically.

Coffee break was over and they shuffled back to work. Lindsay was stationed at the filing boxes for the second morning rotation — inserting slips for books signed out and removing slips for books returned. There was a telephone on the pillar to one end of the table.

As Lindsay sat filing, she was thinking about the phone.

She got up from her stool, walked over to the pillar, and called the Royal Alexandra Theatre. She was nervous.

'John Dawes here.'

'Mr. Dawes?'

'Yes.'

'This is Lindsay Flynn calling. I don't know if you remember me?'

'Of course, Lindsay. It's nice to hear from you. Your call is quite timely, actually. We were just talking about you. Have you landed another job?'

'Why do you ask?'

'The truth is we have six people we want, but only five spots to fill.'

Andy *must* be one of the others, she thought. How could she not? Though, maybe she's not! Lindsay's mind raced. *What was this about?* Was Jesus Christ a bondslave to prophecy? Did the words of Isaiah, Jeremiah, and Ezekiel exact every action, every thought?

'Yes, I was calling to decline, with sincere thanks for your having me in. I had another offer and thought I'd better grab it.'

'Is it a role you think you will enjoy?'

'Oh, yes! Thanks. I'm very happy about it.'

'Wonderful! I hope you will try us again in future, when we announce a call for applicants.'

'I will, thank you! I am touched you would say that.'

'It was sincerely meant. Goodbye, Miss Flynn.'

'Goodbye.'

As she put down the phone, Lindsay was immediately confounded. She sat down on the stool.

'That wasn't it,' she told a fistful of transmittal slips.

5

Lindsay didn't go straight home after work, even though she was anxious to know what Andy had heard from the Royal Alex. She could have called from work, of course, but she didn't want to hear her friend's fate over the telephone. She hoped the director would not mention her having called to decline. No, he wouldn't. If he had, she'd tell Andy she'd decided against, after thinking it over.

She preferred not to have to say anything to Andy about it. It wasn't much of a sacrifice if she didn't really *want* the part in the first place. She felt self-righteous and stupid.

Her detour brought her down to the second-hand bookstore on Spadina, just below College Street. She wanted to find something about Exeter, especially its cathedral. She'd browsed around the library stacks that afternoon and discovered a history of the war-time air assaults on the city: a whole book about the bombings!

She hadn't had the same luck with the church. The library didn't usually acquire the kind of thing she wanted — one of those glossy colour picture-pamphlets one finds in the local gift shops. If, however, any Toronto tourist had *ever* brought one back from an Exeter holiday, she thought, it would end up in this store.

The shop, tightly packed with books up to the ceiling, with surplus piled on the floor and heaped in boxes all down the back corridor, offered a wonderful selection.

Lindsay liked the owner. He was reliable, soft-spoken, and kind. Not strikingly handsome, but he had a certain charm that made him a magnet for attractive women. He had a pretty assistant who came in on Saturdays, and a perfectly beautiful daughter who helped in the store from time to time. Even his patrons seemed to include an abnormal number of women of physically fortunate birth. Lindsay was among these, although she had a certain obtuseness about her appearance that forbade her noticing.

'Hello, Len!' she said, coming into the store. The owner was seated at the sales desk at the front, busily pricing the persistent mountain of books.

'Hello, there,' he replied, wishing he hadn't forgotten her name. 'Lindsay.'

Len smiled broadly and said, 'I do try to remember, but old age takes its toll!'

Lindsay asked if he had anything about Exeter Cathedral. Len directed her to a stapled spine on a shelf toward the back, behind the store's central partition.

Lindsay's mind was electric as she pulled the skinny blue pamphlet down and looked at its cover. The shelves with their rows of colourful jackets dimmed to soot and smoke wisping through the air. She stood on the comely iron footbridge crossing the City Wall out past Cathedral Close.

Around to the north, outside the wall, things were relatively undisturbed. She passed an anti-aircraft gun-pit and thought how out of place the Choirmaster's sensitive face would seem among the artillerymen.

Coming back into the city past the Post Office, Lindsay could see most of the city had been smashed to rubble.

Along the High Street, very little was still standing; or, if something was erect, it was due to the support of mounds of broken stone and brick piled at the foundation. Like the sloped drifts of scree at the foot of young rocky mountains. Some of the rent structures here and there still resembled buildings, having visible remnants of walls, windows, and doorways.

The soot and smoke issued from the many fires still burning. The bells and horns of fire brigades could be heard all around, swelling with shouts, the clanging of shovels, and the noise of army vehicles.

A path had been cleared along the High Street. She didn't have the proper shoes for it, and her feet were becoming sore from the impact of the sharp stone edges on her soft plimsolls. People were coming and going right and left as she walked along the narrow boulevard. Some were digging for those fortunate enough to be alive; others loaded the dead onto the beds of trucks and into vans. She saw several men with white civil defence helmets. They wore rugged greatcoats, some with bags or backpacks over their shoulders. Some held spades, others had radios. A few carried bundles of hammers, ladles, and spanners.

Gelignite Jacks, Lindsay thought. Gelignite Jacks carried hammers, ladles, and spanners.

She hadn't seen an unexploded bomb yet, but she knew there were never many to be found, especially after a saturation bombing like this. Should one land unexploded, another coming right after would often set it off.

It had been such a beautiful city! She could not reconcile the indifference of war to beauty, and life. It was strange, she thought, how nature did *not* seem to be indifferent to beauty. It was more indifferent to life. It was certainly indifferent to genius.

Lindsay saw a Tudor half-timber merchant's house standing forlorn as she made her way along; its ground-level gallery, crammed with antiques for sale, was undisturbed. She saw that Guildhall — a pillared Gothic monstrosity — had also escaped destruction. A few blocks further along, another fortress was largely intact. 'Tuckers' Hall,' according to its sign. She didn't know what a tucker was, except it had something to do with cloth or weaving. Nobody in there to ask about tuckering today, she thought.

She found herself marking her steps by the surviving structures, trying not to think too much about the death and devastation. This is like the cinema for me, she thought. It *is* horrible, but it doesn't really *touch* me. I don't live here. I haven't lost my family, or my estate. I won't be returning from a week's stay in Bristol — or from active service — to find my parents or children reduced to cinders, my house to gravel.

Coming around the corner from Tuckers' Hall, she passed the parish church of St. Mary Steps, another survivor. She stood below the mechanical clock high up on the streetside tower wall. King Henry VIII and two javelin men in coloured miniatures, surrounded by a carved canopy. The clockface itself, with only an hour hand, was decorated with carved figures representing the seasons. She noticed the clock-hand rock ahead a notch, still keeping time. The lives of the people here will also creep ahead, notch by notch, recovering.

She walked further along, feeling no urge to return, vaguely wondering if her roam was conducted in any way. She repeated her belief they usually were, and, almost immediately, around a bend in the road west of the City Wall below St. Mary Steps, she saw it.

The bomb. Two civil defence workers. The unmistakable depth of *his* eyes beneath the rim of a white helmet atop the body, astride the bomb. An arm bringing a great hammer down to the casing.

Before she could panic, before she could shout, before she could understand, the set was struck. Evaporated. Vanished.

The great gelignite wind from the blast rolled toward her in slow motion, in expanded time, whipping up dust and debris. It slapped her face, crushed against her chest, lifted her feet from the ground, and hurled her back several yards from where she had stood. She landed, dazed, in the blown-away atoms of iron, stone, and Gelignite Geoff Douglas.

'Lindsay! Are you okay?'

The smoke and soot cleared to reveal a number of giant dustballs along the kickboards at the base of the bookshelves. Len was leaning over her, fanning her briskly with an old *Life* magazine. A customer had donated a light jacket, which Len rolled up and placed beneath her head.

'Yes. I'm sorry for the fuss. I must have fainted.'

'Shall I call a doctor?' He didn't actually know where or how a doctor could be called anymore — but a hospital was close by and, if necessary, he would gladly have taken her over himself.

'No, I'm fine. I'm just very sorry for the trouble.'

As Len helped Lindsay to her feet, she recognized the man who had donated the jacket. He worked for the U. of T. Libraries, at Technical Services on Pears Avenue. He had taken Lindsay to hospital in a taxi once before, in late July.

'You'll be thinking I'm always falling over, Michael!'

'Oh, gosh! It's you! Are you sure you're okay?'

'Yes, thank you,' Lindsay said, 'just lack of air, I think.'

Getting to her feet, she marvelled at his appearance, as she had the first time they'd met, when she'd fallen on the stairs at the Planetarium. He had the longest hair she had ever seen on a man, down almost to his knees, a silky strawberry-blond colour. He wore a black vest over a skin-tight shirt sewn from puckered fabric in muted psychedelic colours. Most striking, however, was the perfume he wore. Strangely evocative, as though it elevated aromatics to some rarefied level; as Lindsay's *seeing* was, so to speak, to ordinary vision.

'Did you read the book I gave you?' Michael asked, making conversation. He'd left Lindsay at Emergency with a copy of Huysmans' *Against Nature*, Robert Baldick's translation of *À Rebours* in a Penguin.

'Yes, I did, thank you. It was pretty heavy going in parts, but quite rewarding. I can't *imagine* the research it required.'

'Huysmans' contemporaries were surprised, too. He was, however, widely respected as an art critic — the leading critic of the day, I gather — so he was known as having a good knowledge of the arts and culture beforehand, at least. It was something of a double life, mind you, as during the day he worked as a clerk in the French civil service.'

'That's interesting.'

'I've tried to emulate des Esseintes' tastes somewhat.'

'Huysmans' hero — or anti-hero — had refined tastes, all right; but, I hope you noticed how the book finished. "Lord, take pity on the galley slave of life" . . . How does it go? . . . "no longer consoled by the beacon fires of the ancient hope." In short, des Esseintes' synthesis exhausted itself. To zero.'

'Here,' Michael said, 'try this one.' He handed her a book of poetry. *An Astonished Eye Looks Out of the Air* by Kenneth Patchen. 'He was quite brilliant. He passed away this year. It's too bad.'

'Thank you — and thanks also for recommending George William Russell before. I found a copy of *Homeward Songs by the Way* at the other bookshop, up on College. His vision was quite profound.'

'Yes, quite,' he agreed. 'A kindly man — poet, novelist, statesman, theosophist . . .'

'And painter. He could see the *sidhe* — the fairies — too. He painted them.'

6

Lindsay arrived home to find Andy asleep, her door open.

She sat down on the bed, and roused her with a gentle shake. Andy's eyes crept open and met Lindsay's.

'I got a part in the chorus.'

Lindsay didn't think she sounded as excited as she should.

'I'm sorry, Lindsay, but he didn't say anything about you.'

'That's okay. I have my sights set on the Lyceum.'

'On *Gelignite Jack*?'

'Yes, especially *Jack*. I'm *really* happy for you.'

She was. A Zen story that Lindsay had read flashed through her mind: A blind Zen master listened to the *heart* with which people extended their congratulations and similar sentiments; most, he found, had envy or resentment mixed with their praise.

Lindsay knew that hers would have been found sincere.

'Lindsay — I've just noticed how *red* your eyes are! Is everything okay?'

'I was down in the used bookstore on Spadina. I saw Geoff's death. I was blown off my feet by the blast.'

Lindsay hadn't realized how upset she was until that moment. Like coming out of shock, to find an emotional backwater lying in wait.

She started sobbing. Andy took her in her arms.

They remained on Andy's bed, holding each other in a silent embrace. Lindsay was comforted by her friend's warmth. Suddenly, she was *aware* of Andy's body there, so close to her. They had never been lovers, Lindsay thought, but they might well have been if love were its only essence. As it was, both brains were engineered for men.

'Will you be able to see him again, before his death?' Andy asked.

'Yes, I think so,' Lindsay replied.

'I hope so.'

Lindsay wondered if this was the tragedy Geoff meant. She didn't think it was. She knew from the start how he would die.

A few minutes passed in silence.

'I'm very glad you got the part, Andy.'

'It's only a spot in the chorus.'

'It's paying work in a big musical at a major theatre. I don't think it will sink in — that you're a part of the big show — until it opens. Then, you'll walk by the theatre, see your picture on the marquee posterboard, and think, "Hey! I'm *in* this show!" It will be *you* singing and dancing for hundreds of people every night, coming out at the curtain call to cheers and applause. *Bravo! Bravo!*'

'I guess it *won't* hit me until we're underway; but, never mind, I *am* thrilled. Don't pay too much attention to what I say otherwise. My mind's spinning.'

'I understand, Andy. Don't worry.'

'Thanks, Lindsay.' She gave her friend another big hug as they sat on the edge of the bed.

'Let's go down and cook some supper. Toast and macaroni calls!'

'Tonight I have a surprise for you! I'm going to make crêpes, for dinner *and* dessert.'

'Wonderful!'

'Yes? I have some interesting fillings. Beef-and-vegetable stuffing for the entrée, strawberries and cream for afters.'

'Amazing!'

Andy's cooking more than lived up to its promise. After they'd finished, back in the corridor between their rooms, Lindsay thanked her again for the treat and renewed her congratulations on the part.

Alone in her room, Lindsay reflected on her circumstance. She didn't think she could be doing much better than she was, having come out cold to a strange place. She had a tolerable job, with few demands attached to it. The university was Mother Earth to its employees: she took care of you, with no threat over your head — provided you were never in neglect of duty and didn't steal.

Lindsay cringed and put the thought out of her mind.

She gazed up at her diminutive home. Her single bed along the wall. The door. The desk, dominating the centre of the space. A small built-out closet covered by a curtain at the far end. Opposite the foot of the bed against the wall, a bookcase.

To her landlord's dismay, Lindsay had painted the walls a colour he didn't like — a sort of raisin-mauve — which he found dark and cheerless. For Lindsay, it was rich and restful.

She got up, put her clothes in a pile on the floor behind the closet curtain, pulled on a short nightie, and changed her briefs, before resting in bed with another of the Lyceum scripts. She had to get it read, as she had an appointment at the theatre the next day for an audition. She had to know what she wanted. In being given the scripts, she had already passed the résumé review and could try out for any one — or all three — of the plays.

Her pillow fluffed up, she started reading. It was the story about the motorcycle racer, *The First Trial*.

His name was Eric Fernihough. 'Fair-neh-hoff,' Lindsay said out loud. His motorcycle was a Brough Superior. 'Broff,' she said. Fernihough took it to Hungary in 1938 for the record attempt. He crashed and died horribly on the first run. She remembered that T.E. Lawrence had also been killed on a Brough Superior.

The cover for the script had been prepared by a professional artist and offset-printed. Its layout included a photograph of Fernihough on the machine. Lindsay recognized the rocker-box cover from her father's garage. J.A.P. Same as the Morgan she had remembered the other day. Lindsay knew J.A. Prestwich supplied engines to several other manufacturers, mostly for motorcycles, like Brough. A popular choice for the high-powered racers of the day, too.

She stared at the photo and examined Fernihough's features closely. His eyes. The details of his face. His innocent, slightly aristocratic, little-moustached English smile. A smile she'd seen in the old newsreels on TV, on the faces of young men in the trenches during World War I, about to go over the top. Unaware, uncaring, or denying their imminent deaths. A 'pip, pip' kind of smile that described how fortunate they were to be civil and English in a world crowded with barbarians. Fortunate to be astride incomparable British machinery.

She looked closely at the visible engine parts — the cylinders, the pushrod tubes, the heads, the supercharger intake. She knew what everything was from watching and listening to her dad. His fervour was infectious — though mostly she joined him there because she loved him deeply. The garage was simply the best place to spend time together. Pretty much the only place. He *spent* that time with her, too. When Lindsay was with him in the shop, her father was warm and talkative, telling stories, explaining what he was doing, and listening. He was eager to know what she had done that day, what she was thinking about.

If a serious matter of any kind arose during the course of their conversations, he would stop mid-motion — whatever he might be doing. His eyes would focus off into space and he'd ask her to tell him her thoughts, slowly and carefully. He would then offer his best suggestion, or his most sagacious observation.

He once tried to teach Lindsay some hands-on technique. A sad smile came to her lips when she recalled the experience, as she inspected the photo of Fernihough's racer.

It was she who first expressed an interest that she might do something. Her Dad said, 'Fine!' He handed her an aluminum rod about two feet long and said they were going to bring the engine on the bench to top dead centre. It was a J.A.P. methanol engine for Speedway — a specialty the company dominated for three decades. Lindsay got muddled trying to follow his instructions, however. Uncharacteristically, he became frustrated in turn and suggested they abandon the effort.

The precise shape of those engine parts stuck with her, with greater moment than any other hardware she ever saw in the garage. She readily identified Fernihough's as the same.

Andy heard her softly crying as she left the bathroom.

She knocked gently on the door.

'Are you okay, Lindsay?' she whispered.

Lindsay got up and let Andy in.

'I just got thinking about my dad,' she said. 'Even after a year, it still hurts.'

'Of course it does. I don't think anyone *ever* gets over the death of somebody so close. It's the hurt of all that love inside — and you'll *always* love them.'

'I just wish I could have been there.'

'You couldn't have done anything about it. There was no warning. The doctor said it was a freak.'

'It's so ironic — sometimes I can see for miles, across time and space, but I couldn't see that my own father was going to fall over dead.'

'Never mind, Lindsay. It's not like you're to blame for anything.'

'I know.' She gently bit her lip. 'I just got thinking about him, reading this play about the motorcycle.'

'Perhaps you'd best not audition for that one.'

'You're right, Andy. Thanks.'

7

Lindsay had stolen a book from the library that morning.

She'd returned it again that afternoon.

Earlier, it had been disturbingly ironic — before Andy came to the door — to realize how recklessly she had put herself in jeopardy. Only 'neglect of duty or theft' could disrupt her sheltered livelihood at the university library. *So, what do I do?*

It wasn't even for herself. It was for a friend. Someone she wished to have as a friend. She'd met him in a nearby coffeeshop a month or so before.

It was the book she was reading that prompted him to introduce himself. He apologized for the intrusion, saying it was a genuine rare book she had there. He recognized the paper, typeface, and binding as being unique to an Irish small press of the arts and crafts revival. Lindsay didn't know a thing about the history of printing. She was interested in drama. For her, this was a book of W.K. Magee's, a schoolmate of Yeats, later a friend of Russell and George Moore. It was a reminiscence about Irish theatre — especially the famous Abbey Theatre in Dublin — and sketches of Sean O'Casey, Lennox Robinson, and others Magee knew and saw there.

46

The man said he had a collection of rare books with an emphasis on Irish literature around the turn of the century. He had recently mortgaged his house to buy the dedication copy of Yeats's *The Secret Rose*, inscribed to George William Russell.

Lindsay didn't know what that meant either. The idea of books as valuable *objets* was completely foreign to her. But, if he needed this book of Magee's, the library certainly wouldn't miss it, and he would be touched by her offering. Her selfless effort on his behalf.

She was disappointed, almost distraught, when his face fell to the floor instead. She showed up at the door, having rushed out and down into the subway at lunchtime and, two stops over to Christie and four doors up the street, he invited her in.

'I have to be getting right back to work,' she said, still catching her breath from the sprint. He was pained to tell Lindsay he couldn't use something covered with stamps and stickers. A library copy no longer had any value.

His anxiety explaining its worthlessness hurt the worst. She could see he *wanted* to be touched and grateful. But he could not. There wasn't any corner of the conversation into which a speck of goodwill could be swept. Their mutual embarrassment was exaggerated by their *wanting* to know each other on the one hand; but sensing, on the other, this inopportune first visit bode poorly for any future possibilities.

'I wish you might have just come for lunch,' he said awkwardly as she left, 'you'd always be welcome.'

She hadn't even handled the *theft* very well. She'd snuck the book past the guards in her jacket lining. So easy to spot, so obviously a theft. Gave her the willies to even think about it. Had she just checked the book out, she could later have removed the sign-out slip from the file. Simple. Could even pass as an honest mistake.

I did this to myself. *Needlessly*, she thought. Believing it was a kindness. Sometimes a little knowledge can just about take your face off.

She settled down to sleep.

There was a concert in Trinity College Chapel the next evening after work. A chamber ensemble made up of students from the Faculty of Music performing Tudor and Jacobean composers in a series. That night it was Byrd, Tallis, and Weelkes.

Andy came down with some sandwiches at six o'clock, and they ate together on the grass behind the Old Observatory, in front of Hart House. As happened each year, they'd been told, the cannon displayed on the rise had been painted bright pink.

'A hazing ritual hosted by engineering students,' Andy said with mild scorn, 'whose imaginations seem to be limited to their own sexual apparatus.'

As they were finishing, the carillon bells in the Hart House clock tower rang out.

'Isn't that lovely! We're lucky to hear a few minutes of this. They aren't sounded often.'

'I've met the woman who plays them,' Andy replied.

'I remember. Telling you about pounding the hammers with her heavy leather gloves. That was fascinating.'

'She said there's only half-a-dozen people in the world who can play them.'

'There can't be too many instruments available to play!'

They both loved Trinity Chapel.

'I'd like to be married here, Doc, *if* I get married,' Andy said as they made their way over to the college.

Entering the chapel, they passed groups of divinity students, all wearing their long black vestments. Lindsay wasn't clear what it meant to be a divinity student. She thought she must stop in and ask one of them sometime.

'They have singers performing tonight,' Andy whispered when they were seated.

No program was printed. One of the ensemble introduced the players, the selections, the original antique instruments, and the five singers in their sixteenth-century parts: treble, mean, countertenor, tenor, and bass. The first piece, the announcer said, would be Tallis's masterpiece, *Salve intemerata*.

Lindsay was carried away as they played and sang. It was truly the masterpiece promised — not only melodic, but with a complex framework, alternating duets, trios, and full sections. Building to dramatic tension, releasing, building again more fully.

No wonder Vaughan Williams was so moved to write his own masterpiece, *Fantasia on a Theme by Thomas Tallis*. She had *seen* Vaughan Williams once. A handsome young man. Thin lips. Dark eyes under dark eyebrows. He was wearing a woolen waistcoat, a shirt with a starched straight-collar, and a loose-knotted woolen tie hanging below the collar corners. He didn't seem to know what to do with his hair, one curly shock in particular dangling in his eyes, reminding him that bit of grooming wasn't going to leave him be.

She sought that *Fantasia*. She ran the theme through her mind and looked. It was still a chapel, but not Trinity. Not Exeter. Gloucester, someone said. The same person continued.

'One is never quite sure whether one is listening to something very old or very new. It is full of visions that have haunted the seers of all times.' An aristocratic voice. Slightly pompous.

'A *seer*,' she said. 'That music haunts me, I can see him there.'

She hadn't yet found a comfortable definition for her ability.

He must be a critic. This must be the Three Choirs Festival, when it was first performed.

She was relieved the critic could neither see nor hear her. That remained something unique to Geoff, and Erin. To Exeter.

She knew the music well; she also knew its sublime brilliance was not recognized at the début. Within twenty years, however, it was thought by many to be one of the great works for strings.

Funny how that worked, she mused. Imagine! Ralph Vaughan Williams *ever* being thought inadequate. We expect so much more, so much faster, so much younger.

She wondered if *this* was the disappointment she had to reconcile.

The players remained seated, but the performance was finished. She would return another time to listen. She watched them all, full double strings and a quartet, folding their music.

Lindsay could see Andy was entranced listening to the ensemble. Her face was taut with concentration and pleasure. The first time, Lindsay had to coax her to come out; since then, it was Andy who ensured they attended every other week.

The Trinity recital finished with another Tallis, a treble motet.

After it let out, they were all the way up to Bloor Street before one of them spoke.

'Beautiful,' Andy said.

'Yes.'

'How about a toasted fruit-loaf and a cup of soup at Murray's? My treat.'

'Okay! It's a deal!'

The restaurant was in the Park Plaza, on the corner of Avenue Road and Bloor. Before going in, they walked along the side of the building where the hotel jeweler's shop had a row of tiny display windows. They were changed each week — always imaginative, always interesting. The valuables had been taken in for the night, but the decorations could still be seen. The theme that week was True Crime. Handcuffs. A model .38 detective special. A cigar case and clipper. White carnations. A porkpie hat. In the morning they would be readorned with a marvelous wealth of gold and gems.

8

The next morning, Lindsay lay in longer than usual. She didn't have to go to work, exchanging the day off for the following Saturday shift. She was expected at the theatre at eleven.

It was another beautiful morning. Coming out the side gate, she went around the front of the house and headed up Bedford Road toward Dupont. She crossed the street in front of what she called the 'weird' place, its front garden full of sculptures and junk. A sign in front announced 'NORMAN ELDER GALLERY,' but she could never work up the nerve to knock on the door. It didn't *look* like a public gallery. She had been told Norman Elder was an artist, eccentric, and adventurer.

She cut over along Bernard and walked up the top of Admiral Road, passing by what she considered the prettiest houses in the neighbourhood.

The theatre was a few blocks further down, housed in a renovated industrial building, previously a factory of some sort. The walls inside and out were aged brick. The narrow forward portion of the structure was three floors of small offices — used by the theatre for administration — with the space immediately adjacent to the front entrance on the lower level serving as the box office. Beyond that, the bulk of the building was one vast open space. Its metal roof, supported by heavy wooden beams, was thirty feet overhead. A tubular lighting battery was suspended from the ceiling beams, winched up and down for convenient movement of the many spot and flood lamps attached, or for changing bulbs and colour gels.

All of the theatre's work took place here, in the space they called the 'hall.' There were no separate facilities for rehearsals, no distinct studios for dance. Permanent elevated flooring for seating, like a terraced hillside garden, had been built in a large semi-circle around the stage. Patrons were seated on plastic stacking chairs — reasonably comfortable for the sort — arranged in rows on the various terraces. A small director's booth had been built out from the third-level offices, up above the seats in the back corner, where lighting and sound were controlled. The spacious main stage was elevated about five feet — sufficient to accommodate an old-fashioned prompter's chute and footlights. In the foyer there was a trio of century-old limelights the original promoter had scrounged when the theatre first opened. Nobody had yet been bold enough to attempt to light them. They were a charming relic, Lindsay thought, like discovering a ship's telegraph beside the major-domo's desk in a seafood restaurant.

Helen was front-of-house manager at the Lyceum. Lindsay always went to say hello to her first. Helen had both nothing and everything to do with the artistic success of the productions. She was the heart and soul of the operation. She kept the shows running — the heartbeat at the centre of its various larger, ever-trembling limbs.

'Hi, Helen!' Lindsay called, hopping up the short circular iron stair — another charming relic — to her tiny office.

'Hi, Lindsay. I'm glad you could come out for this. I'm your fan!'

'Thanks, Helen. That's very sweet. I'll do my best.'

'Are you going to try out for all three?'

'No, just *Gelignite Jack*. I didn't really like the female character in the Michelson play, and there's only the one significant role to choose from. The other play wasn't right for me.'

'Sure, I understand,' Helen said, 'it's only one audition anyway. Martin's directing one of them himself and, as house producer, persuaded the other two guys to conserve everyone's energies by sitting down together to see the actors who passed the first cut. We've got to watch every nickel.'

Down in the theatre, a young man was delivering a pained soliloquy from Albee's *Zoo Story* to the panel of three seated in the front row, paper-packed clipboards on each of their laps.

Appointments had been scheduled over fifteen-minute intervals, but early-comers could sit in the theatre and watch. There was no other place to have them wait. Lindsay quietly made her way over to some chairs in the back where another woman was sitting.

When the man was done they could talk for a few minutes.

'I'm Lindsay.'

'Hi. I'm Suzanne.'

'Nice to meet you, Suzanne. You're auditioning?'

'Yes, for *Hail, Holy Light*. I couldn't make the schedule for the first play about the mystic. I'm working a job now, with about ten weeks to go.'

'That's great!'

'Truth is, it's my first paying role. Over at the Colonnade. It's not a big part, but I'm also understudy to the lead. I've been called up three times for it thus far.'

'Lovely! What's *that* like?'

'Not that great, really.'

Lindsay could see this woman had 'star quality.' She may be just starting out, she reflected, but she possessed the natural radiance usually seen in the actors finally cast. Obviously, a director could see it too. That's what Andy meant the other day, about 'knowing.' It was as though an audition was hardly necessary, except to confirm the performers had the technical skills they said they had. Otherwise, they could spot one of their own a mile away. They *could!* They did.

'The trouble with being an understudy is that it's very trying, emotionally. People sometimes leave the theatre saying how they had "only" been able to see the understudy. It's heartbreaking!'

Lindsay was moved. It might be her. It probably would be, soon.

'But, I am committed to this thing. It's a matter of inner conviction: To know that you have *chosen* theatre and, even if that choice may be *wrong*, to think that it is *right*.'

'I'm terrified sometimes.'

'Me, too. You're always having to reinvent yourself, especially in terms of continuing to be successful — which *only* means sustaining a steady income.'

'I have a day job,' Lindsay said.

'Once you get going you won't be able to keep that. Then what? I see brilliant people in their forties and fifties who still have significant financial concerns. It fills me with despair and worry.'

'But you stay with it!'

'I have no choice.'

'I understand.'

'If you understand — and I believe you do — then *you* have no choice either.'

Martin Henry called to Suzanne to come down. It was her turn to perform.

Lindsay thought for a minute about the last point Suzanne had made. She was touched by the truth of it.

It echoed what the artistic director for drama at the college in Calgary used to drum into them. 'It has to be something you *have* to do,' he would often say. A lot of the students thought he was too hard on them, but Lindsay appreciated the rigour. 'Some people think I'm too tough,' she remembered him telling her once, 'but that's our job. You shouldn't have come here if you want less. We're a trade school. We train *performers* — and we push them, too! Here, you *learn* to perform. It boils down to hard work — and drive. Talent sustains you, but it's drive and ambition first.'

She wished these ideas might also have some greater significance — to Geoff's portent — but nothing leapt to mind.

Suzanne was delivering a monologue from *A Midsummer Night's Dream*: 'These are the forgeries of jealousy . . .'

Lindsay knew it by heart. She called Shakespeare's work 'The Great Divide.' Broadway was a significant challenge, but didn't offer the difficult language, the sheer volume of dialogue, and the exceptional demands of Shakespeare. The lead roles entailed learning more great poetry than most *literati* commit to memory in a lifetime. And the pressure! The precedent of tens of generations of inspired performances gone before.

When she was done, Suzanne collected her coat — left on the chair — before speaking briefly with Lindsay.

'What say you, Titania?' Lindsay said warmly.

'I do not doubt but to hear them say, it is a sweet comedy.'

9

Lindsay was in despair as she left the theatre.

'What the hell am I doing?' she asked a parking meter. 'You invest the whole of your energies — talent, drive, research, and desire. And for what? A career laden with fear, anxiety, insecurity, and relocation.'

'So, what is the reward?'

'Who's that?' Lindsay said with slight alarm.

'Erin.'

'Erin?'

Lindsay turned. Erin Powell was sitting on the grass beside her. She thought it must be a public garden.

'Hello, Lindsay.'

'What did you just say?'

'I said, "So, what is the reward?" I'll tell you — to be *deserving* of success, even greatness. "'Tis not in mortals to command success, But we'll do more, Sempronius; we'll *deserve* it."'

'That's from Joseph Addison. *Cato*.'

'That's right. See? Even by that, I know how deserving you are.'

'What do you mean?'

'Lindsay, you have not *learned* drama, you have *assimilated* it. You will not be conscious of that, of course, especially when surrounded with talented friends.'

'Just Andy, and the others at the library.'

'There must be many artists among them — young people, intelligent and abundant with energy.'

'Yes, that's true.'

'This "star quality" you talk about sometimes is not a matter of beauty, talent, intelligence, *or* experience, although it does *require* all of those things. It is similar in kind to what you said to me about singing. It must be inborn. Then, that essential raw material can be worked.'

'How do you know so much about what I've been thinking?'

'Let's just say, whereas you can sometimes *see*, I can sometimes *hear*, if you like. I'm a singer after all!'

Lindsay said nothing for a moment.

'Do you know Geoff Douglas well?'

'I know that Geoff can hear, more consequentially than me. He can hear the voices of angels. When Geoff instructs the choir, he strives to draw from them what he has heard on high. The music, when the anthems are his to select, are written by others he *knows* have recorded the seraphic song.'

'I think Vaughan Williams heard the voices of angels when he wrote his *Hodie*. That was *exactly* my thought when I first heard it. He was there. You *know* he was there.'

'Vaughan Williams? You must mean another of his works — or the Palestrina?'

Oh! Lindsay thought. Vaughan Williams' Christmas cantata wasn't written until 1952, when he was eighty.

'Um . . . It's something you might hear. Sometime.'

Erin smiled and winked.

'Have you seen Geoff since we last talked?'

'Yes, I have. I told him I saw you in the empty church, hoping he might be there.'

'Did he think that was silly?'

'No, not at all! Why do you ask?'

'Because I don't know what he's like. I know his name, his career, his history, even his death' — Lindsay looked Erin in the eye, to see if she might have said something wrong. Erin just nodded, so Lindsay continued — 'but I can't understand a thing when it comes to his *personality*.'

'No. You will probably not know him in that way. For some people, he is his music; for others, he is a man of simple, even taciturn, speech, and gentle manners. You mustn't expect to know any more than that.'

'He's not *trying* to be mysterious, is he?'

'Goodness, no! There are many of us who have had few friends, whose feelings are remote from other people.'

Lindsay blushed.

'You have no cause to feel ashamed, Lindsay, when your heart has been full of love.'

'What about . . . .' She stopped herself. She decided she could not ask about Geoff's visitors, even if Erin did know her thoughts.

'I hear what you *extend* to me, Lindsay. Not what are, in earnest, your private feelings. The angels, even — or above all — would not invade your privacy. As for Geoff, all I know is that his heart is pure and loving. Nothing more.'

'Are you in Exeter to sing?'

'Geoff wants me to sing. A private concert at the cathedral. The tradition of the church prohibits women singing in the regular service, you see. I do love Geoff, but I only have so much voice to go around. It's all I can do to keep my voice up for paying engagements. I could not come in and sing for the organist at Exeter Cathedral on a caprice. I'd have to take three or four months off.'

'Why don't you suggest to Geoff he *make* it a paying concert — a recital — at the church? I'd be surprised if the Dean and Chapter objected to raising some extra money, especially with a famous performer.'

'That may be an idea, Lindsay, thank you.'

'It seems important to him.'

'It is, and there's no knowing what might be prompting him. His are usually sound impulses.'

'Can I ask you one more question before I go?'

'Of course.'

'Do you ever perform music you don't like?'

'Why would you ask me that?'

'I auditioned for two plays. I think I may be refused the role I want, but awarded another I don't like.'

'If the song doesn't "sing" to me first, the performance is a crashing bore.'

'Though you'll still do it?'

'It takes much greater discipline. Because there is no love.'

'But it's love that makes your performances evocative,' Lindsay said. 'Music, like poetry or drama, has a kind of stored magic. You can't reveal that magic without love.'

'If I don't feel that I *deserve* to be out there — that I can do a good job and have something to say — then I *don't* belong there. A part of being deserving is a belief in myself — that I *am* good, and that my soul comes through in my singing. Whether or not the latent magic will be revealed for the audience I cannot know — except by their response.'

'It must be very exciting when you find that you have electrified an audience.'

'Tell the directors which roles are *you*, Lindsay — and go electrify your audiences.'

'Goodbye, Erin. Thanks.'

Lindsay was cheered being with Erin, but that passed in a trice once back on the dusty Dupont sidewalk. She did not have cause to go back into the theatre, nor to tell them anything. She did not know *what* they were considering her for — if anything — except that Martin had asked a question about how she'd handle some dialogue in the Michelson play, *Hail, Holy Light*.

She did not know if she was an actor.

Lindsay was too upset to walk home, too upset to stay where she was, holding the parking meter. Besides, a bald guy had pulled up in an old Vauxhall Ventora and, in a second, he'd want to deposit his dime. Lindsay went down to the café where Karen worked.

Happily, she was in, serving sandwiches to the lunch crowd.

'Lindsay! You look all beat up! You drink tea, right? I'll bring you a strong one. And a doughnut — on the house.'

'Thanks, Karen. I'll pay for it.'

'Never mind — but do tell. What's up?'

'Oh, I've just had an audition at the Lyceum.'

'I thought so. You're looking about average, for someone who wants the part. No — let me guess. You don't think you got the part you want, but you think they want you for one you don't?'

'Was I talking to myself out on the sidewalk?! Those were exactly my thoughts, almost word for word.'

'I've been pouring coffee here for six years. I've watched three theatres along this stretch come and go. Over that time, I've seen this look in people's faces more often than I can count.'

Lindsay managed a wan smile.

'That's reassuring, Karen.'

'It's meant to be. Remember, an actor — a capable one — never knows what might be going through the casting director's mind. And you can't second guess them: *so don't try*. Look, that guy over there? He knows. Hey, Howard! Come over here!'

Lindsay suddenly felt shy.

Karen detected her hesitation, and told Lindsay not to worry. Howard was long and happily married.

'Howard, this is Lindsay. Lindsay is an actor, new in Toronto.'

'I did the drama program in Calgary,' Lindsay offered.

'Good for you! I think Calgary — and Edmonton — will be great theatre centres in Canada soon.'

'Howard's a fifteen-year veteran. He's performed all over.'

'Wow! You're famous!'

'I don't think I've ever been *famous*. Certainly, actors don't become famous in Canada. Here, they are *employed*.'

Lindsay laughed, knowing he was exactly right.

'But you've had work in the U.S.?'

'Yes, on Broadway no less. For ten years steady.'

'I can see you've had a successful career! That's really something; although, outside of the business, nobody will ever appreciate how difficult it must have been.'

Lindsay paused, sensing she might learn something from this person; but, again recalling Geoff's caution, didn't want to appear exploitive. Best to be direct.

'Do you mind if I ask you for some coaching? I could use the advice. I feel so lost sometimes. Like, right now.'

'Sure thing, as long as you don't mind if I sound a trifle pedantic.'

He swallowed a big mouthful of tea, as though to warm up the speech centre in his brain.

'To get anywhere, you must *perceive* yourself as a business, and organize an information system. You have to spread your net wide, researching and knowing the plays that are coming up, knowing what roles you can perform. You've also got to let the directors know. They must hear from you regularly, and see you at auditions and around the theatres. Then, when they're looking for someone, they might think, "What about that person I spoke with in the café that day?" That's how it works.'

Karen poured them both a fresh cup of tea.

'I'm not sure how you can measure success,' Howard continued. 'Twenty years ago I thought: If *only* I get to Broadway, I'll have made it. The big time. Within five years, however, I was *on* Broadway in good roles. I began saying to myself: Oh! Is *this* making it? Is this the pinnacle of my theatre career? It's tough to keep driving yourself.'

'You're not trying to discourage me, are you?'

'No, not at all! I can see you have the right bones for it. Honestly. All I'm saying is that as the years go by, you may find you have to branch out. Produce. Direct. Maybe do some writing.'

'Howard has done all of those things, and all brilliantly.'

'I've written *one* play which ran six weeks at a repertory theatre in Vancouver. Big deal!'

'It *is* a big deal, Howard,' Karen quietly insisted.

'When you're directing, how do you know you've got the right person for the part, Howard?'

'That's a good question. A lot goes on instinct. It's the first round that is agonizing, when we only have the résumés. The last show I did, in Vancouver, we *narrowed it down* to eight hundred applications to *screen*. Ultimately, we wound up auditioning four hundred people for twenty roles. What if I lost the best person because they didn't put their height on a résumé?'

'I guess you have to be psychic, Howard,' Karen said dryly.

10

'This theatre business is a terrible emotional rollercoaster,' Lindsay confided to Brian. She'd gone over to the Periodicals Reading Room with some magazines that had been returned to Circulation. The departments were adjacent on the main floor of the library. Technical Services was upstairs, the book stacks three floors below.

'I don't envy you at all,' he said. 'My goals are more modest.'

Brian was studying hand bookbinding. Most of the leading experts in Canada were living in, or nearby, Toronto.

'I'm not sure about that!' Lindsay replied. 'You're an artist and a craftsman. That's just as public.'

'I guess,' he responded — trying to think how he could be supportive. 'But I can work and improve my skills without needing the immediate approval of others. You need to sell your skills before you can improve them. On the surface, that sounds like a Catch-22. You can't get work until you're good, but you can't get good without getting the work. The saving grace is that the theatres *do* hire new talent. If they didn't, the industry would shrivel up in no time.'

Lindsay thanked Brian for his counsel and, seeing it was her break time, went down the stairs to the first book stack, 'A' floor, where, off at one end, the coffee room was located. Another woman joined her as she walked along. They had never really spoken, and now merely exchanged courtesies. Her name was Linda. She was very attractive, nicely dressed, always wearing a flattering musk perfume. There was a melancholy about her. Not that she wasn't cheerful — she generally was, and friendly — it was something deeper. Lindsay wished she could become her friend, perhaps even contribute to relieving her disconsolate air.

Thinking about Linda in this way brought on a reflective mood in Lindsay. Instead of going to the coffee room, she turned around and walked to the far edge of the floor, to the study carrels that lined the windowed walls of all three levels of the book stacks.

Graduate students applied for the use of these cubicles so they could keep books on hand for personal use on the shelf above the work table, but which were still available for other library patrons to access.

Lindsay sat in an empty carrel off in a corner. Even though they were only painted sheet-metal against the stone wall, the enclosures had a monastic cloistered charm for her. She stared out the window, across the park by the Old Observatory to Hart House.

She wanted to talk to Geoff.

She envisioned the library window, surrounded with stone, as panes set in the wall of Geoff's stone cottage.

Her heart pounding, she knocked on the door. The sun was bright overhead, but she did not know whether she had arrived at the right time of day. She hoped her inner self was conducting things properly. She could not bear any humiliation. It was hard enough already.

Geoff opened the door and, with a gentle smile, extended his hand.

'Hullo, Lindsay,' he said.

She took his hand and said, 'Can I tell you a story?'

'Please come in,' he said. 'My home is modest, but comfortable. Come into my study.'

Geoff was as kind and assuring as anyone could be. Lindsay was nervous in the extreme.

'Please, sit down. A cup of tea?'

Lindsay wasn't sure if he knew why she was there. It dawned on her that his having friends visit in this way was not clandestine. This was someone who heard the songs of angels. For him, it was conversation — learning, and opening his heart — to be of help. It was the touching that caused people to think it might be covert. Sitting there, the idea of the mystic resting against her body did not seem threatening or unnatural to her.

She was still nervous.

Geoff served tea. His study was brightly lit, lined with tall bookcases, all of a sumptuous dark-coloured wood. The walls and ceiling were panelled with the same wood. He asked her how old she was, about her mother and father, about where she'd been raised.

After a few minutes' chat, he got up and asked if he might sit beside her.

Lindsay nodded her assent. Geoff motioned to her to move over a little on the settee.

'Do you want me to take my top off?' She was wearing a soft woollen turtleneck.

'My friends do what suits them,' Geoff answered, 'what mood, closeness, or bond they might want or need.'

He paused, only briefly. 'Stay just as you are, and tell me your thoughts.'

He rested his head on her shoulder, his cheek just leaning on the one side of her bosom. He gently laid his hand on her arm opposite.

Stories do get blown out of whack over time, Lindsay thought.

'I find it hard to know what to believe,' she said. 'My life seems so disconnected. I have a specific objective in sight, but in an area that, almost by definition, results in a fragmented life. Notwithstanding that, I just wish I could make a start! That is, just having some sense of going from job to job would be *something*, even if my life was even more of a patchwork. Painters can just sit down and paint. I cannot just stand up and perform. Well, I could! But, what I mean is, to really be involved, you have to get *work*. An actor out of work is only somebody calling themselves an actor. If I just felt I were getting a start.'

She didn't want to confess she had bungled her efforts to understand and fulfill his charge after they first talked. It was too much to add on top just then. She had first to remedy her goals. Then, she would see her other destiny more clearly.

'As it is, I should be called an auditioner rather than an actor. I think there are a lot of people who do nothing *but* audition the whole of their vain careers. They never learn how to perform for real audiences, night after night. I mean, you'd wonder why anyone would *want* to be an actor. People don't realize how hard it is to do the same thing night after night. After all, they only see the show once. I might do it five hundred times — I only wish! I just want a *toehold*. Whatsoever else, I believe this is my calling. I believe I *belong* there. I know I do.'

Geoff sat upright beside her. He gave her cheek a stroke, brushing aside a few tears that had escaped while she spoke.

'Young people cannot know the *meaning* of their youth,' he said, 'an unfortunate ambiguity.'

He saw Lindsay to the door.

It was already about fifteen minutes into the second morning shift. Fortunately, she hadn't been placed on any of the public service desks. She resumed her duties in the microforms cage with no notice taken of her absence.

Lindsay was quietly rewrapping some film spools when, to her surprise, Andy came in.

'Kathleen told me you were down here.' Andy's expression was lively with excitement. 'Guess what!!'

'Martin Henry called?!'

'Yes! Yes yes yes! Congratulations! *Gelignite Jack* starts rehearsing *next week*. You have the female lead! The singer friend of Jack's.'

'The LEAD! Oh, my God! I'm stunned. I'm truly stunned.'

'That's not all, Lindsay. Two other feature players also have day jobs, so they've decided to rehearse evenings. All the performances are evenings, as well, except for weekend matinées.'

'That's fantastic. *Thanks*.'

'See you at home!'

The rest of the afternoon and evening breezed by for Lindsay, buoyed by the tremendous relief of having made tangible progress.

Andy and Lindsay curled up on Lindsay's bed before retiring. They'd had their evening baths, and were sipping hot Ovaltine.

'We're both working! Just like that,' Andy said. 'I'm *so* pleased, *so* excited. I was so worried about getting a start.'

'I couldn't have done anything without you. Your friendship made it possible.'

'*I* feel the same way. I don't think it's the first time in history two friends prodded each other along to great things.'

'It is a wonderful start.'

They punctuated their mutual congratulations with mouthfuls of the hot drinks.

'Andy.'

'Yes?'

'I think Geoff Douglas may have had a hand in my getting this part. I saw him today. I talked with him about it. It was much simpler and warmer than the playwright suggests, by the way.'

'He may have been thinking nice thoughts for you — and that may matter — but he didn't do three years with the Young Canada Players, two years of college, and everything else. Nor did he pass that audition. You did! You know that. Sure as plonk *he'd* be the *first* to know. So, if he helped you do something you hadn't *earned*, that would be wrong. If, however, he — or anybody else — helps you along when you have put in the real sweat ahead of time, there's nothing amiss, right?'

'Right, but . . .'

'But what?'

'I think I may have had the genie come out of the lamp and offer me a wish — but then I wished for the wrong thing.'

'What do you mean?'

'It's like — you get so focussed on some immediate objective, you lose sight of other, more important, things.'

'I'll sound like your dad, but you have lots of time to shape and round out your life any way you want.'

'Yes,' sighed Lindsay. 'That's a big part of what I was trying to say. It's also doing the right thing at the right time.'

11

'Geoff?'

Lindsay had come around the side of the cottage, finding him in the back garden.

'Can I talk to you?'

'Of course. Come in. Would you like some tea?'

When they were seated in his study, Lindsay was flushed and teary. She pulled off her sweater to a tank top, and held Geoff's head to her.

'I only realized when I got what I wanted that I didn't get what I wanted at all,' she said. 'I mean, I *did* want it! But there's something else more important I need to do — or would like to do — first.'

She sniffed back her tears.

'It's something nobody *else* could do, so I can't really think why *I* should be so privileged. But then, I don't think anybody really cares. I don't think *nature* even cares. Nobody cares I'm here now, or that I'm *able* to be here now. We are all locked inside ourselves, and no one really knows, touches, or bothers too much about our inner lives, moment to moment.'

She let out a deep breath.

'My dad died suddenly a year ago. I was off at college. I never got to see him. He was just gone. I know there's no magic to bring him back. I don't want that, anyway. He had his own life to live, his own relationship with God. I just . . . just . . . .'

Lindsay was trembling, holding back her tears.

Geoff sat up.

'Most people would find it tedious to relive their lives,' he said.

'But most people want to relive their lives with the benefit of the knowledge and experience they've already acquired from living. I only want to be aware of *one* specific thing that I wasn't before — even if it is wholly subconscious or intuitive — to know, just before the time comes, I must go home. To say goodbye.'

'And all that you have gained? Your present way of life, your happy circumstance, your friends, and your emerging career?'

'Some things you have a *lifetime* to build — or not, but for the grace of God. Other things, once missed, offer *no* other opportunities. Whether your life is otherwise long or short.'

'Will you wish, then, to recover from *every* error in this way? To have a second chance at every stumble, to patch every bit of folly?'

'*Of course I will*. Everyone does, in some way or other, I think. This, however, is about my *father*, who vanished suddenly to the grave.'

Lindsay paused to catch her breath. She genuinely didn't mean to seem persuasive with Geoff.

'Surely that must be something apart from ordinary day-to-day bung-ups? Even if it's not, I think nature, or God, or whatever, is unconcerned about the progress of these minutiae anyway.'

She understood what she was saying only as love. She could not conceive of any other possibility.

'As well,' she continued, 'however brilliant I might be, whatever else might be in my heart, whatever I might achieve, sooner or later I'm going to get blown to bits, or run over by a truck, or my heart will up and quit. Then, my wishes — fulfilled and not — are vanished. So, nature has no more than fifty or sixty years to wait before every shred of evidence is gone.'

12

The halls of the college were clean, that particular clean seen only in schools closed for the summer; whose staff scrubbed, waxed, and polished everything in sight over the three-month hiatus.

Lindsay had arrived in Calgary the day before from her home in Vermilion, Alberta. She wanted to be an actor. She wanted a *career* as an actor — she'd done three seasons with the Young Canada Players to test the theory — and this was where she would get some good training to get her on her way.

As much as she was pleased, she was equally frightened and lonely. Waiting for the registration room to open, Lindsay found herself offering a friendly smile to another newcomer standing there with her, one who also welcomed a friendly face in the crowd.

'Hi! My name's Andrea — though everybody calls me Andy. I'm from Stettler. I've come here to learn this singin'-and-dancin' pizzazz!'

'Hi,' Lindsay answered, beaming, almost laughing out loud, and taking Andy's hands in hers, 'I'm Lindsay.'

The doors to the room were being opened.

'Let's get going, Lindsay! It's showtime!'

Apostrophe

If the women don't find you handsome,
they should at least find you handy.

RED GREEN

1

'No trucks,' Harold said aloud, leaning against a post at the mine gate.

The gate, a waist-high light barrier made of steel tubing, was rarely closed. There wasn't much traffic to control in the isolation of North Baffin.

Harold had been waiting at the airstrip earlier in the day when someone suggested he come down to the mess hall at the mine for something to eat.

He said he would, provided he'd be able to get a lift back to the strip later on. Although Nordair stepped up the schedule to twice a week in the spring, Harold was eager that he not miss this plane. 'There'll be lots of trucks coming up here, never worry,' the miner assured him.

'No trucks,' Harold said again. He knew in his heart that the promised convoys would materialize later, closer to arrival time. He was anxious, however, and wouldn't feel secure until he arrived back at the terminal.

The building was too small to call a terminal, really. Too small to call a building, for that matter. But it was heated, and often slept twelve or fifteen people if a plane was weathered out. Which was frequent during spring and fall, when the sun rose and set, and the changing weather tended to produce fog and cloud. In the summer and winter — when the sun was, respectively, ever present or ever absent — the weather was more stable, and flights more reliable.

Fortunately, it was only fifteen below, and Harold was dressed in his full cold-weather regalia. A heavy down parka with snapped inner wind membranes, overtop a woollen liner from an Arctic-issue air force flight suit, overtop thermal underwear, with regular army mukluks on his feet. A two-piece hood covered his head, the inner, resembling the Red Baron's leather flying cap, snapped under the chin. His hands were protected with heavy beaver-skin gloves, which pulled up almost to the elbow and were fastened to the parka with leather cords, like the stringed mittens he had protested against throughout elementary school.

Harold cupped his mitts against his face to melt some of the ice gathering on his beard, the result of his own breath condensing and freezing, the moisture from which he wiped away as well as he could with the glove's furry backs.

Standing there, he remembered coming home from his winter tour three months before, packing a narwhal tusk and a musk-ox hide. Even after three years of thirty-day visits four times a year — always at the solstices and equinoxes — the temptation to bring back souvenirs was strong. He had dressed the hide himself with salt in the back room of the co-op at Grise Fiord.

Usually the first stop in the south was Montreal. That time it was Toronto, and he had booked a room at the old downtown guest hotel, the Prince of Wales. He could picture the shock on the face of the desk clerk when he came into its elegant lobby in his Arctic gear, carrying the tusk in a seven-foot length of plastic pipe and the musk-ox in a canvas duffel bag. The ox was beginning to melt, and blood was seeping through the fabric. Putting down his American Express card, Harold said to the clerk, 'I hope you've seen those TV commercials, about when you don't look your best?'

It didn't appear to Harold that he had.

I could always walk, he thought. This was the only road in North Baffin, apart from those within the hamlets. Twenty-four miles long, it connected the mine at Nanasivik with the Inuit community of Arctic Bay. The airstrip, built to service jet traffic — 727s with gravel gear — was off the main road about four miles along.

'I might as well, if only for something to do,' he said aloud.

Harold knew there were no polar bears about. They tended to stay close to the ice edge out in the strait this time of year; and, besides, that morning at the guest lodge some hunters had returned, bitterly disappointed, having failed to find a bear anywhere in the area. The guides, one white exile (any white resident seemed to Harold to be an exile from the south) and two Inuit, were contrite. The Texan visitors had each paid thousands of dollars to get there, equip themselves — including custom-tailored caribou coveralls — and buy their permit tags. Sure as hell, after all that, they wanted those tags pinned to a dead bear's ear.

The road wound through the coastal hills. It was sufficiently steep at first that Harold found it tiring, wearing his heavy clothing. The land was a rolling moonscape: barren, littered with broken rock, silent.

So very, very silent. It *seemed* quiet in the villages — but that was like a riot of noise once a distance away, out in the open. Harold had experienced this before, travelling with Inuit hunting seal, or, once, going to the glacier northwest of Grise Fiord. This time, however, he was alone. There were no vehicles. No sleds. No baggage. No ocean. No seagulls. Silent.

The blood rushing by his eardrums made a metred, *whooshing* sound. The brush of his nylon sleeve against his jacket filled the air with tone and rhythm, like a ponderous chorus of strings in a concert hall. As he moved farther from the mine, over the succeeding hills and rises, the silence deepened further. He began to notice a hum in the air which he realized, with a start, was the electrical activity in his own brain.

Then, without thinking, he turned and looked for the train. Anyway, he *thought* he heard a train, a steam engine. At first a casual gesture, like paying incidental notice to passersby in a shopping mall, the action aroused greater interest when, of course, there was no train to be seen. He realized with amusement that it had been an aural hallucination. His subconscious mind could not tolerate the extreme silence, apparently, and had recovered a few decibels from the archives — whatever was at hand — to fill the gap.

Harold glanced skyward as he walked along, smiling about the train, and noticed four giant ravens circling at a tremendous height overhead. The birds typically had immense wingspans, often five feet across. These were at least that large, or bigger — circling, circling, gracefully gliding, waiting. Waiting for Harold to fall over dead from exposure, or to get torn up by a bear, at which time they would happily pick what they could from his bones, whatever remained.

And then, a genuine sound. A truck, after all.

A half-ton pickup, painted the familiar Department of Transport yellow. Harold could see the vehicle approaching about half-a-mile distant, across a narrow valley past a bundle of hills.

He put out his thumb.

The driver, a weathered older man, stopped for him. Harold got in, smiled, and they drove on. It was normal not to talk at first. Inuit historically spared no energy on verbal courtesies, a mannerism which exiles increasingly acquired as the years went on, especially if they had never returned to the south.

After a time, the man spoke.

'Don't get too many hitchhikers up here.'

Harold turned and gave him a friendly look.

'Been up here since 1957. Twenty-five years. And, in fact . . .'

He paused, briefly darting dark eyes toward Harold out of an expressionless face.

'. . . you're the very first one.'

2

There were half a dozen people sitting around the terminal when Harold arrived back.

'Hi, Harold,' came a voice. It was Bill, a Petro-Canada geologist and an old acquaintance. 'Look at this,' he said, pointing to the Arctic

Petroleum Operators' Association magazine he was reading. 'Dome has been testing an Archimedean Screw Tractor. I knew the idea was being considered, but didn't think they'd actually build it!'

'I don't understand what it is,' Harold said.

'You can see in the picture. See?' He showed Harold the page. 'The tractor sits on two aluminum screws, like a pair of giant corkscrews laid flat, side by side. To move, the screws are rotated, driving the vehicle over the ice. The screw drums are also buoyant, so it can go through water. The turning blades act like propellers.'

'That's quite something!' Harold said. 'Right up there with the General Dynamics submarine tanker.'

'Yeah, that's a hoot. Of course, this is a hundred-thousand-dollar project, while that's a billion. They'll find, of course, that icebergs are a bigger problem below water than above.'

Bill returned his attention to the magazine.

'I'm looking forward to the plane today. I think a friend of mine is coming up,' Harold said.

'Who's that?' Bill asked.

'Valerie. My old friend Valerie.'

'A woman, coming up here?'

'Sure, why not? I grant you there's not too many about in these parts, but hardly zero. Most of the miners are here with their wives and families, for example.'

'That's true,' Bill conceded.

'Now, being past forty, I may be getting a little jumpy,' Harold said, 'but I figure I'd better do something about settling down.'

'Inviting your friend Valerie up here is a start toward settling down?' Bill asked, and laughed. Harold laughed in return.

'No, I suppose not. It's just been off again and on again, that's all. I couldn't come back down now, so I suggested she come up.'

'You'll have to pay extra for a room in Pond Inlet.'

'John won't charge me if he's not full. Or, if the Hawker-Siddeley is in, she can bunk with the stewardess. They always guarantee her a women-only room. Anyway, those details are the least of my worries.'

Bill noticed that the percolator had shut off. 'You want some fresh brew?' he said.

'Too cold to stand outside to drink these,' Harold said, folding a dollar into the receipt cup.

'Who is this friend of yours anyway?'

'Someone I met a couple years ago, at the Glencoe Club in Calgary. I was having lunch with my boss when the sales rep from the printing company came in with her sister.'

'We all know you guys are the publishing barons of frontier oil and gas,' Bill said.

'It was love at first sight.'

'With the saleswoman's sister, you mean.'

'Of course. It was an almost mystical experience.'

'For you or for her?'

'Quite right!' Harold replied, taking his meaning. 'Not only did she fail to notice me; but, as I tried to get to know her, she took me for a nutcase.'

'Why would she think that?'

'Oh, you know how it is. I was nervous. Like a schoolkid. I never knew I could be so awkward, so high-strung.'

'Yup,' said Bill, his interest waning.

'I'm just back from two weeks in Grise Fiord,' Harold said, detecting Bill's declining humour and changing the subject.

'What was doing up there?'

'We just about put the Twin Otter down the hard way, on the ocean ice, coming in. You know that airstrip is very short, even for STOL craft, so it's always like a rodeo landing there. Except this time there was also a sudden fantastic updraft off the glacier and we were flipped up and over, just like you'd toss a coin. Then we slipstreamed upside-down, dropping fast toward the pack-ice, wailing like a dive bomber!'

'Holy shit,' Bill whistled softly, imagining himself there. Anybody flying in the Arctic knew it might be them next time. Everyone came up the following season to find a pilot gone. A friend. The pilots were friends of all the regular travellers. This spring it was Bob, who went through the ice landing on a lake in the Mackenzie Valley a few weeks before. Everyone loved Bob. He looked like Howdy Doody. There was an air of innocence about him.

'It was Thompson flying, with Randy-the-Lady-Killer. Thompson's pretty much the toughest heart you'll find up here. But, you should have seen him when we got down. White as a sheet. And they had to pop Randy out of the co-pilot chair with a bottle opener!'

Bill laughed.

'Took them several hours to recover. I know that because they had other charters from there over the next two days, so they stayed at the hotel. I tagged along on the first trip — a wildlife survey along the Devon Island coast.'

'How'd that go?'

'Great! We saw dozens of whales, some musk-ox, and a couple of polar bears. They slowed right down for them, full flap at about one hundred feet. Next day, they flew off to pick up some Thule, the native Greenlanders. A cultural exchange with the Inuit, they said.'

'Right!' Bill observed. 'That's like Jews and Arabs in Palestine getting together for a square-dance. I'll bet that was something. Were they wearing their polar bear knickers?'

'Yes, they were! I was stunned when I first saw them. I have a carving of a Thule in bearskin pants that I got in Pond Inlet a while back, but I didn't know they still wore them!'

'Only on "cultural exchanges," I think,' said Bill.

'The pants went from their calves to just below their armpits. They were bare-armed and otherwise bare-chested. It was ten below, too! The sun was out, at any rate.'

'I couldn't live like that.'

A voice came over the public-address system.

'It's like they need a bloody speaker system in here,' Bill quipped sarcastically.

'Nordair has reported mechanical problems, and will be keeping the aircraft at Frobisher Bay overnight for repair.' The distinctive deadpan voice of a native person.

The waiting passengers, by then swelled to twenty-six bodies, all groaned in harmony.

The groan ambled out the door and floated skyward, an appeal to the heavenly hosts.

3

The road to Arctic Bay was hair-raising. It wound a perilous path over and along rocky ledges, up and down gullies, hardly a friendly inch the whole way. Harold was riding in the taxi — an old Inter-national Harvester passenger truck — with Bill, Duncan (another acquaintance), and three other delayed Nordair passengers. None knew if there would be room at the guest house. 'You can always find a place to stay, somewhere,' the driver told them.

They got talking about the circumstance of the Inuit in the Eastern Arctic.

'The situation is complex,' Harold said. 'I generally don't like to talk about it. Besides, any tough talk has to come from Inuit. Said by a southerner, it's perceived as bigoted rubbish.'

'Which is what it probably is,' added Bill. 'They've seen "expert" after "expert" come from the south, spend a few weeks, go back, and write a book. They resent that. They feel their destiny is being shaped by busybodies who don't know their inner feelings, their way of life.'

'The same way mine is down south!' Duncan replied. 'Shaped by busybodies in government who establish policy on my behalf whether I like it or not. And, don't tell me it's a democracy and all that. Every four years we elect a dictatorship.'

'Their way of life cannot be preserved as it was,' Bill stated. 'The people here know that. In fact, that's not the issue: it's self-determination. Self-rule.'

'I think self-rule would result in more responsible behaviour,' Duncan responded. 'At the Indian Affairs meeting in Pond Inlet last fall, it was Inuks standing up to complain that their own youth were terrorizing the environment — tearing up the tundra with snow-mobiles, mowing down the caribou, and so forth. It's all in the published minutes.'

'Pride for the environment will only emerge with a tangible stake in the game, which means native government,' Bill returned.

'Who's going to send up twelve-hundred gallons of fuel oil per person per year then? As long as the communities are the ward of the federal government, all that stuff is free,' Duncan pointed out.

'The "communities" were the federal government's idea in the first place. The people were herded into hamlets against their will, often to areas where there was no wildlife, occasionally placing clans who had been hostile for centuries in the same village, and, originally, the people were numbered! Wasn't till Abe Okpik went around on the naming project in the late 1950s that government records were switched over.'

'He got an Order of Canada for that,' said Harold, lying low on the sensitive issues.

'Sure,' Duncan interjected, 'but do you know what all that was for? Not the natives' benefit. It was for sovereignty. To protect Canada's claim on the islands.'

'These are complex concerns,' sighed Harold, as they came in sight of Arctic Bay.

The community was built at the apex of the bay, a slow semi-circle of pre-fabs stacked up the hillside six or seven streets deep. About five-hundred people lived there — a dozen-odd white exiles, the rest Inuit. Of them, the majority were children and young people. Since the nursing stations had been established fifteen or twenty years earlier, newborns were surviving with much greater regularity, and the hamlet populations had grown rapidly.

Harold and his companions got out of the taxi at the fuel-storage tank beside the power station. Electricity was generated with two massive v-16 diesels housed in a large sheet-steel garage. All of the hamlets had them. The structure was black with soot, and exhaust smoke and steam from the engines poured out into the cold air. A rumbling nightmare from William Blake's vision of the industrial revolution, Harold thought.

Harold's knowledge of the arts and literature distanced him from many or most of his peers working in the north; but not, generally, from Inuit. He had a frank and honest bearing about him. Whereas southerners tended to be suspicious of his dark eyes, the locals responded with trust. They valued their clear penetrating quality, someone once told him, and also that he always looked a person in the eye. Harold had made a special connexion in Arctic Bay on his last trip, the news of which spread overnight throughout the Eastern Arctic, among the Inuit.

It was during a community meeting, where, essentially, the Elders gathered to roast southern PR men, enabled by simultaneous English and Inuktitut translation. They had all been through the motions dozens of times before, through dozens of meetings.

This time, something unusual happened. Harold responded to a lengthy question before the translator had given the Inuktitut into English. He knew what the man had said, having heard it several times before in other meetings. He didn't even notice what had happened. The Inuit did, however, to a person. It was a sensation. Language is the bond of culture, Harold thought afterward.

A dog team was being harnessed out on the ice. There must be some tourists in town, Harold mumbled to himself. They'd better bundle up warmly! The land was almost clear of snow, but there were still two or three metres of pack ice on the bay. The land possessed a different schedule of seasons than the ocean, because the tundra heats and cools more quickly than seawater. In late spring, tiny tundra flowers often began to appear on land, while the sea remained covered with thick ice. Then, in the early fall, when the land was bitter with snow and ice, the water was open offshore.

Up the hill on the main street Harold and his friends ran into Frank, the settlement secretary. Frank was an exile from Nova Scotia who came up north in the mid-1960s, married an Inuit woman, and stayed.

'Hi, Frank.'

'Back already, Harold! I heard Nordair was grounded.'

'Yup.'

'Not too much going on here tonight.'

'Like my life,' Harold joked. He didn't mean it, as with Valerie probably coming up he felt there was plenty going on.

'Maybe you should go back to Nanasivik,' Frank replied. 'The "Spring Breakup" starts tonight. The company has brought a musical revue troupe from Toronto.'

'Good thing they weren't coming up today,' Bill said.

'I don't know where we'd stay,' Harold added. 'There's no hotel at the mine, and I don't think the taxi will bring us back here to Arctic Bay late at night. Besides, it's pretty costly.'

'That's the main thing,' Duncan said. 'I think that John Hembroff would put us up. I'll call him on the phone. Can I use yours at the office, Frank?'

'No problem. Harold, why don't you and Bill head over to the Ventures? I think one of the theatre people is there, buying some carvings. Another couple is just going out for a dogsled ride. Pretty cold for it, mind you! I guess they figure they won't have many other opportunities.'

Frank and Duncan walked off to the hamlet office. Harold and Bill went the other way, toward the store.

'Funny thing, you know, Bill.'

'What's that, Harold?'

'Yesterday morning I was talking to Frank. He had just arrived back from an overnight trip to the ice edge, where Inuit are hunting narwhal and whatnot. He gave me an Arctic char the size of a British bulldog, which Kenn Borek is carrying down to the Pacific Western freezer for me.'

'That's nice.'

'That's not what I was getting at, though. He was telling me how they built an igloo, which they slept in — about how much skill it took to build, and how warm and comfortable it was when they were done. You should have seen the sparkle in his eyes! He was genuinely delighted to have done this thing. You'd think, after so many years here, the thrill would be gone.'

'Just like a kid again, was he?'

'That's it exactly! *Just* like a kid.'

'I haven't felt like that for a while.'

'Me neither. Jaded, I guess.'

Coming in the store they saw Jake, the sole employee, and waved hello. Most of the stores in the hamlets, apart from the Hudson's Bay Company, were co-operatives. This one was privately owned.

'So, how come the body of water is Hudson Bay, but the store is Hudson's Bay?' Bill said to Jake with a smile.

'You ask me to solve the competition's metaphysical problems?' Jake jokingly protested in return. 'What are you bums doing back, anyway? Nordair not come in?'

'Grounded in Frobisher,' Harold said.

'These will do nicely,' came a voice from the back room. A man emerged carrying a pair of walrus tusks.

'Okay, that's great. I'll get those written up and find you the wildlife papers. Oh, this is Harold West and Bill Hutch. Harold and Bill, Alex Kempston.'

'Nice to meet you, Alex,' Bill said. 'Where are you from?'

'Originally from Jasper, Alberta, believe it or not, but I'm living in Toronto now. I'm general manager for the revue performing at the Nanasivik mine this week.'

'Kempston, from Jasper? I know a Kempston originally from Rocky Mountain House. Valerie Kempston. Are you related?'

'Small world, I'd say! Sure. Valerie's my cousin on my dad's side. How do you know her?'

'We've been dating. I think she's in Frobisher, waiting to come up with Nordair tomorrow.'

'Really?' Alex stalled, 'I saw her in Calgary a few weeks ago, but she didn't say anything about it.'

'No, we just made arrangements last Thursday, over the phone,' Harold said.

'Right. Wait a minute! — Harold, we had lunch together before, didn't we? When was it? Two years ago anyway. I was the one who made the insensitive joke about the troubled child.'

'What was that?' Bill asked, always interested to know of any insensitive comment he might reuse.

'Valerie works as an occupational therapist for young people. At one o'clock she said she had to get going. She had a patient at one thirty. What's his problem? I asked. Neglect and an inferiority complex, she said. Have another beer! I said. Everyone laughed.'

The humour of the exchange went over Bill's head, but he laughed anyway, rather than give himself away.

'Well, I'm glad you've worked out your problems. I gather she wasn't too excited about you at first,' Alex recalled.

'No, I didn't deserve any better. I grew somewhat obsessive,' Harold replied.

'I'm glad you can see that now, if you don't mind my saying.'

'No, I don't mind. I roll my eyes too, looking back at myself.'

'I guess we all have some lumber in the closet to roll our eyes at,' Alex said sympathetically.

'Not me,' Bill replied.

4

Harold was persuaded to go back to Nanasivik, to see the chorus-line, and stay over with Duncan's friends.

The minesite was always neat as a pin. The housing estate in particular humbled the other hamlets on Baffin Island, littered — as they usually were — with broken-down snowmobiles, fuel drums, and other industrial clutter. As well, at Nanasivik the houses were attractively painted — with colours other than white, brown, or aqua — and had nicely finished details.

The mine itself lay between the hamlet and the coast of Strathcona Sound, about a mile further down. There wasn't much evidence of the digging, except for various paths and roadways into the hillside. The ore was carried down to the storage building on the sound in giant trucks, each as big as a house, with eight-foot-tall tires and ladders up to the cockpits. The ore storage barn was among the most capacious enclosures in the world — although dwarfed by the biggest, the Boeing aircraft plant in Washington — having to store a full year's production on site for the brief fall shipping season. Painted bright red, it was visible for many miles from the air.

The focus of the townsite was the community centre, a spacious, well-designed, recreational complex, executed in steel. Adjacent to that was the 'dome,' a large open mess hall, which is where the three went first.

'They feed you like lumberjacks up here, don't they?' Bill said.

'Most of these guys might as well be lumberjacks,' Harold replied, 'for the muscle they put on.'

'I put on twenty pounds each tour,' Duncan said, heaping two-pounds-odd of pork chops, potatoes, and turnip onto his plate.

'Everyone is very friendly,' Harold said.

They sat by themselves at a table in a corner.

'Do you ever feel that you wasted away your youth?' Harold asked the other two.

'Where did that come from?! Apart from weeks on end in this bleak place, maybe! You worried about women, Harold?'

Duncan had a certain flair for practical insight.

'You know what they say, Harold. When you first get up here — the very first day — look around for the most degenerate walking lump of female flotsam you can find. The day you find her looking sexually attractive, it's time to go home!'

It was a crude joke. Bill laughed anyway.

'I guess I *have* been worried about women, but not like that. You have a lot of time to think things over up here.'

'Most guys up on research tours, like us, find they're sleeping eighteen hours a day to pass the time. You know, you get your work done in a week — a busy week, mind — but then have to wait another week or two for a plane. And sometimes those are chained, village to village. You might have days or weeks to pass in two or three or more places as you go,' Bill said.

'Especially in the winter,' Harold added.

Harold could see that he was not going to draw either of his companions out in the way he hoped. He didn't finish his dessert. Bill and Duncan fired up their persistent argument over northern land claims, between gulps of coffee.

Just as they had, once again, exhausted the topic, Alex Kempston came in for dinner with three young women. Harold waved and, after filling their dinner trays, they came over to join him.

Bill and Duncan said they were going to Hembroff's to play cards, ensuring that Harold knew the house number — saying goodbye before introductions could be made.

'Are they coming to the show?' Alex asked.

'That's hard to say!' Harold replied. 'I hope you won't be disappointed if they don't make it.'

'No, of course not. The place will be packed anyway. The full-timers living up here really look forward to it. It's a long dark winter!'

One of the women had been looking at Harold, conspicuously trying not to stare.

'Oh, that's rude of me,' Alex said, noticing her glances.

'Harold, this is Heather Wexler, Julie Hagen, and Lindsay Flynn. The stars of our show. Ladies, meet Harold West.'

They exchanged nods and greetings.

'Do you live in Nanasivik, Harold?' Heather asked, now unself-conscious about looking at him.

'No, I'm from Vancouver, but living in Calgary. I'm a technical writer in frontier oil and gas, up here doing field work and community liaison.'

'A writer, that's interesting! Do you do any creative writing? You have the eyes of a poet, I think,' Heather said.

'Yes, he does have nice eyes,' Lindsay said pleasantly, for all to hear. 'Dark and mysterious.'

Harold blushed.

'I am very flattered, ladies,' Harold said. 'I'm sure you meet more handsome men than you know what to do with, much less pay a compliment to a tired old sod like me.'

It hadn't quite come out right, but they understood and offered friendly smiles in return.

'Well, we're starting to get on in years,' Julie said.

'And touring these shows for so long,' Lindsay said, interrupting.

'That's right,' Julie continued, 'after ten years in professional theatre, your perspectives change.'

'You start to appreciate a thoughtful person,' Heather said.

There was something *about* Heather. Harold couldn't put his finger on it.

'Well, my experience is that most young women are suspicious of single men — older single men, especially.'

'You can usually tell what's going on inside just looking at some-one. I'm sure you know that, Harold.'

Alex, concentrating on eating up to this point in the conversation, said with his last mouthful of coffee, 'I hate to break up the party, folks, but I think we'd better be getting ready for the show.'

As they were leaving, he turned back briefly.

'Oh, Harold — did you call Frobisher Bay to see if Valerie was there?'

'No,' Harold replied.

If she wasn't there, he didn't want to know.

5

Harold sat in the dome toying with his breakfast. He didn't have much of an appetite, though he knew he should eat. A couple of hardhats at the next table were joking about how the feds had installed flush toilets in the Pond Inlet hotel for the Indian Affairs Minister, the only ones north of Frobisher Bay.

'Hi, Harold,' said a voice from behind.

Harold turned. It was Heather.

'May I join you?'

'Of course you may, thanks for asking,' Harold said. 'I really enjoyed the show last night. I'm a *big* fan of the old show tunes, Jerome Kern, Gershwin, and Cole Porter. It was delightful.'

'I love doing them,' she said.

Harold smiled.

'You look sad, Harold.'

Her tone was tender, but not maudlin.

'Oh, not sad, really,' Harold said, trying to perk himself up. Whatever he was or might have been, it was never a bleeding heart.

'Just reflective?' she asked, a glint in her eye.

'Yes, I suppose you could say that. Thinking about "life." The truth is I have a *good* life — an exciting life, even — but now reaching the middle, I feel a little awash.'

'So, you're going to go out and buy a sports car and paint the town red for a few years?'

'No, no,' Harold laughed. 'I sympathize with guys who go through that, but I've been spared any urge to recover my youth.'

Heather smiled warmly.

'It's a simpler thing for me. I feel like I've been a long time getting here, to a point of professional — and emotional — stability and the like. But, now that I've arrived, I'm not sure what it's for.'

'That's an interesting way of putting it, Harold.'

'I'm glad you think so — sincerely, I am. That perspective came from an old boss of mine, a gifted business manager. Before any strategic planning got underway, he would always ask: "What is this *for?*" He didn't feel that anything worthwhile could be achieved without that concept first being pinned down.'

'These things function at different levels. The question of what "life" is for is complex. It *can* be answered, I think, but only by limiting the context.'

Harold was pleasantly surprised at her intelligence, and at her understanding him the way she did. Direct. Immediate.

'It is all to do with what we believe,' she added, 'and that comes from different quarters; for instance, a biologist or anthropologist might say we're helpless to our genetic code, which is programmed to promote the survival of the species. What values we add on top could be seen as further encouragements toward that same goal.'

'I guess philosophy and religion are a rebellion against that — to clarify *individuals* as significant,' Harold said.

'Significance is a tough issue. My grandad was a gunner on the *Yorktown*, at the battle of Midway. As you probably know, the *Yorktown* was lost.'

'And?'

'No. He didn't get out. Or wasn't recovered, I don't know which. He was a craftsman, a fine woodworker. He was *significant* as an individual. Indiscriminately wasted.'

'Yes, I see what you mean.'

'Regardless, what you say is probably true. The creation myth attached to a culture is usually the giveaway.'

'I find the Judeo-Christian myth intolerably naïve.'

'That's a conundrum,' Heather replied. 'Our social and ethical frameworks extend from the creation story, the same as in other cultures. Which may explain some of your feeling adrift: that myth is the core of an individual's sense of purpose. If you find it naïve, you lose your social mooring somewhat. Your sense of belonging is challenged.'

Harold sipped his coffee thoughtfully.

'When I was younger, I didn't think very much about growing older,' he said. 'Now that I *am* older, it seems like I shouldn't be having to work so hard. But, I'm working harder than ever, and the days pass by in a blur.'

'*The Days Run Away Like Wild Horses Over the Hills*. That's *so* evocative for me. Doesn't it capture the feeling? It's the title of a book of poetry by Charles Bukowski.'

'I like that,' Harold said.

'It doesn't really resolve any of these basic ontological questions, however.'

'That's true,' Harold replied, 'though it helps clarify our needs, which is useful. In pedestrian terms, I think it all must come down to a sense of personal satisfaction. I don't have that now because I haven't made the home I want for myself. But then, I wonder if *that* would be satisfying. When you're young, the range of possibilities is great. The field narrows as you get older. Your options narrow. Your energy diminishes. You no longer have the resources to squander on experimentation and trial the way you once did.'

'Most people make their full investment in their kids. I won't have that opportunity. I cannot have children.'

'So, what will redeem the activity of living for you?'

'*Every* action is a contribution to civilization, Harold.'

6

Harold sat in the library in the recreation centre. Heather had gone to the gym for a workout.

Lindsay came in and, seeing Harold there, sat down beside him.

'Mind if I sit with you?'

'Not at all! Nice to see you.'

'Heather said you two had a deep philosophical conversation.'

'She's a remarkable woman,' Harold replied. He almost said *girl*, but revised his thoughts in time. 'You are *all* remarkable, in fact. And what a great revue last evening! Thanks again.'

'Thank *you*,' she said. 'Without the audience there ain't no show, as they say.'

Harold saw that Lindsay was looking into his eyes quite closely. He averted his gaze.

'I think you have some magic in there,' Lindsay said.

'Had. Once,' Harold said, consciously casting his usual reserve to the wind. 'I haven't thought about it for some time.'

Although she had brought it up, Lindsay was surprised at his candour. Her facial expression betrayed her.

'I figure you either understand or not,' Harold said, 'with our speaking so cryptically.' He paused for a moment.

'Besides, it doesn't matter anymore. Even when I was at my peak, I grew frustrated because I couldn't mobilize those energies whenever necessary, plus my friends acquired expectations I often couldn't fulfill. Now I believe — ironically — it must have *come* from something in that stressed-out, wired, obsessive self I've left behind. It's gone now.'

'It doesn't go away, Harold. It just changes.'

Harold smiled and started to sing, softly, one of her Jerome Kern songs about happier times now long passed.

'*The last time I saw Paris, Her streets were dressed for spring . . . .*'

Lindsay laughed, winked, and said she had to get going.

Harold, thinking along similar lines, wondered again about the airstrip. The jet should be arriving in a couple of hours.

He bumped into Alex in the corridor on his way out.

'How about a coffee in the dome?' Alex said in greeting. 'Then we could get a car up to the depot together.'

'It takes a month to get over the caffeine shock when I get home!' Harold said, 'but, sure, thanks, though I'll have a hot chocolate.'

'You been up here a while?' Alex asked when they were seated.

'Two weeks this tour. Another two weeks to go.'

'What kind of things do you do?'

'Meetings, mostly, with the Hamlet Councils in Resolute, Grise Fiord, Pond Inlet, and Arctic Bay. I also visit the scientists up here and whatnot. I'm the senior analyst for the project, and have to keep the experts on track. That's the official part. I also hitch along on the bushplanes wherever I can, if something interesting comes up. As well, of course, the unexpected usually happens!'

'Like what?'

'Well, for instance, flying from Grise Fiord to Pond Inlet last week we got an emergency call on the radio. I was the only passenger on the plane — a charter leg — but, in any case, a distress call means immediate diversion. A Panarctic Cherokee with small gear had gone down on Prince of Wales Island.'

'The *real* Arctic wasteland.'

'Really! That central core is the Arctic most people imagine. Utterly barren year round. What was *scary* about this trip was that the beacon was working, we had global navigation, and the sun was out, but we couldn't find them! We circled for about half an hour before finally spotting the wreck. Snow had blown over the wings, and it's just a speck to begin with. Imagine if the beacon wasn't working! You'd *never* be found. Never!'

'Were they okay?'

'Luckily, yes. Our plane had skis installed, so we could put down. I'd never landed on deep snow before. Was about fifty *g*s' braking force when we first touched snow! It was goddamned cold too, and these poor guys were executive types with only ski jackets. They were pretty glad to see us. Actually, it was *me* that just about didn't get out alive.'

'What do you mean?!'

'I had to pee, really badly. I walked away from the plane a bit, and dug through all my layers of duds to pull out my dick. Well, it's forty-five below, with a brisk wind, right? The shock of the cold seized me up inside. I just *couldn't* go. I managed to force myself, but it was a trauma!'

Alex laughed, understandingly, shaking his head.

'I froze my feet once in Grise Fiord. Similar kind of temperatures. It was my own stupid fault. You have to take the felt liners out of your mukluks every night to dry them out. Well, I didn't one night. In the morning I threw them on and hopped on the plane, where I added *more* sweat sitting in the cockpit all bundled up. Out into the winter cold and dark on Ellesmere Island, and — Zappo! Feet, socks, and liners *welded* together in one frozen mass. Had to go to the nursing station to have them removed.'

'I'm sure you must have had some heartwarming moments, too.'

'Oh, many. I arrived in Grise Fiord the week they had their TV satellite dish installed. Up to that point they had no broadcast television. Well, I'm talking to some locals at the hamlet hall, and their faces are beaming! Talking about world affairs, asking me what I thought about this, and my opinion on that. Don't imagine I'm being patronizing telling you this. The world had suddenly *opened* in their homes — for better or worse — for the first time. The impact was unforgettable.'

Together they glanced up at the clock. It was time to find a ride to the airstrip.

'I walked half way yesterday,' Harold said, telling Alex what the old man in the pickup truck had said to him. Today the taxi was waiting in front of the dome. Bill and Duncan were already seated.

The driver waited until all of the seats were full before leaving.

'This damned place doesn't improve much with familiarity, does it?' Harold said to Bill when they got inside the terminal. 'Didn't we see this movie yesterday?'

'Yeah, we sure did.'

'When will you be back next?'

'Frankly, I don't know. Petro-Canada thinks there might be some mining prospects on their permit lands, which I've verified, but they're not terribly serious about it. Discouraged by the approvals process, I think.'

'It's pretty tortuous, though more so for oil and gas than mining.'

A quiet descended. They didn't have much to talk about.

'Up in Grise Fiord I made what I think is the longest telephone call in world.'

'What?' Bill said.

'Yes. You know the payphone upstairs in the hotel there? Well, I put in a dime, and called long distance directory assistance. For Hobart, Australia. Asked the operator for the number of the Hobart Sailing Club.'

'Are you nuts?' Bill was not amused.

'Just trying to have some fun.'

'You may need Grise Fiord for the world's most northerly postmark, but not for the longest phone call. The earth is round! You can make the longest call in the world from *anywhere* in the world. From Toronto, say, at about 44°N 79°W, you'd call 44°S 79°E.'

Handy to have a geologist around, Harold thought.

'Well, that probably puts you out in the Indian Ocean. There's not much land in those extreme southern latitudes! Antananarivo, Madagascar would likely be your closest bet.'

'Thanks for the advice, Bill,' Harold said, regretting the mental anguish he'd apparently caused with the original remark.

The plane was expected any minute and people headed outside. They always went outside when worried about the plane landing, regardless of the cold. As though by standing beside the airstrip they might better coax the plane down.

It would *need* some coaxing. It was densely overcast past about one-hundred-and-fifty feet. A G-3, a large turboprop, had gotten down an hour earlier, but it was a different story with the jets. The pilots *would* make their best effort. In poor weather, often three passes from under the cloud. The first quickly to see for themselves they had good visibility at the necessary altitude to make a landing. If they saw they did, they'd circle around and make a practice pass.

Then, the third and last pass. They'd come out of the cloud and if everything was right — their approach, altitude, wind, flaps, and all what-have-you — to make a perfect safe touchdown, down they'd come. If *anything* wasn't right, the pilot pulled back the throttle and away they went. Till another day. The pilots had to be conservative. Safety demanded it.

The sound of the jet was intermittent at first, a kind of distant thunder. But it was, clearly, the jet.

Everyone clapped and cheered.

It circled overhead, poking once briefly below the cloud.

'He's taking a long time lining up his pass,' Bill observed.

Seconds passed, each one an infinity.

The sound went away.

'He's not leaving?!' Harold said to no one in particular.

It got louder again, and appeared suddenly from beneath the cloud. A perfect approach. Perfect.

Put it down! Put it down! Harold was shouting in his mind. He knew they wouldn't.

They couldn't.

Another long silence. A broad circle out of earshot.

Loud again. Closer. Closer. Through the cloud!

'Oh, God! He's overshot!' someone shouted, 'he's goofed it up!'

No one uttered a sound. No groans. No curses. It was over. All present turned and walked away in unison. All, that is, but Harold.

He remained fixed to the spot for some time, gazing absently after the plane.

He drew a deep breath.

'Come back,' he spoke quietly, 'come back!'

He stood another few minutes before turning to find that Heather had walked up behind him.

'Come on, Harold. Let's go home.'

East Fortieth

'Chieftain,' said Pwyll Lord of Dyved, 'if I have
done wrong, I will now earn your friendship.'

THE MABINOGION

1

The house sat on East 40th, just past Victoria. Roxanne had flown out, and took a cab from the airport. Over the Arthur Laing bridge and up Marine Drive. She loved it here. She would have liked to live here, but real estate prices were through the roof, and it was hard to get work.

One by one, the pre-war houses on East 40th were being torn down and replaced with large squarish monstrosities, as on many, many central Vancouver streets.

'Showboats,' the taxi driver called them. His childhood home, he'd said, was razed last year for one. Over on Cypress Street, south of 41st.

Her gramma's house would also disappear soon, Roxanne thought. Last month, the doctor said she could no longer live there on her own. So, what did she do? She had the place painted. Fresh white paint over the stucco. A gesture of defiance. Or denial.

Roxanne was sorry to see it painted. The coloured glass bits stuck in the original salmon-tinted plaster made the exterior interesting. Now it was white, glass bits and all. The last few specimens of genuine untouched Vancouver stucco would probably find their way into museums soon, she thought.

It was a typical arrangement for an old Vancouver street. No cement curbs, mature trees populating broad verges, the grass meeting patchy asphalt in uneven joins down the boulevard. Roxanne stopped in front of her gramma's gate and gazed sentimentally at the sidewalk for a moment. Visiting here as a young child, she was fascinated with the rows of little dimples rolled into the wet concrete when the walks were poured, thirty or forty years before.

She had movies of some of her visits. Super-8s, taken by her grampa, who passed away in 1974. He was a wild man with that camera, which she found amusing at the time, but was grateful for now. He parked the Studebaker along the verge then, before he built the garage in the back garden. Roxanne loved him deeply, especially for the way he loved and cherished her grandmother. If he returned home before she was back from the bakery (where she worked for twenty-seven years), he'd drive that old Studebaker to the bus stop — hardly two blocks away — and wait to offer her a ride home. He was charming, complimentary, always asking her gramma about herself, her feelings, even after fifty-five years of marriage.

'I'm also always asking Gramma about herself and her family,' Roxanne announced to the gate, 'about her younger years in particular.' Her grampa hadn't built the house, but he'd put in the new foundation, the garage, and installed the fences. Roxanne looked closely at his fence: it was made of twisted wire, arranged in overlapping loops tacked into parallel crossbeams, the lower at her ankles, the upper at her waist. So old-fashioned, with a certain delicacy, an elegance even. The showboats usually featured bulky iron rails set between brick pillars. Elegant like Alcatraz.

Her gramma interpreted the order to move as the next worst thing to a death warrant, despite the assurances Roxanne offered to the contrary. On the other hand, if she, a visitor, found each detail so endearing, she could certainly understand her gramma's trauma. This had been her home since 1947. Forty-five years. Six years longer than Roxanne had been alive. Every molecule would have become like a part of her own tissues.

Roxanne pressed the bell, her travel bag to one side at her feet. She often had to ring several times, as her gramma's hearing had declined along with whatever else. If she was watching television, the bell would never be heard. Her gramma always had the volume cranked up. Loud.

The TV was silent, however, and Roxanne heard the latch-lock turn only moments after her first ring. Tina, the housekeeper, opened the door.

'Come in!' she said cheerfully. 'Your gramma's just having me wash and set her hair.'

Roxanne deposited her bag in the front bedroom, to the right of the entry, and came back through the living room, stopping at the panelled-glass door leading to the kitchen. The same sofas and chairs as when she'd visited as a five-year-old. One time, her grampa cooked pancakes for the two of them at ten o'clock in the evening, and they'd sat here together watching *The Thing* on television.

I wonder if other people's grandparents buy new furniture? Or, do they all preserve their belongings unchanging, as an anchor of irrefutable continuity for their children and grandchildren? There was, of course, a new TV. Although her gramma had simply moved the black porcelain jaguar from the top of the original black-and-white set to the top of the new colour model. As though nothing had *really* changed. That's what she wanted when her gramma was gone, she noted. The black jaguar. Oh, and the beer tray she dried her dishes on, and *her* grandmother's mixing spoons.

'Come in, dear,' she heard from the bathroom. Her gramma's voice. Even as she'd aged, and her health had deteriorated, it seemed to Roxanne that her voice had remained the same. It may or may not have, in truth.

'Happy birthday, Gramma!'

'I didn't know it was your birthday!' Tina said with delight. 'How old are you, dear?'

A mischievous smile lit Gwyn's face.

'Seventy,' she said.

They all laughed.

In reality, she was turning ninety-four.

Roxanne gave Gwyn a kiss, telling her she'd wait in the living room.

'Seventy,' Roxanne hummed, easing into one of the well-worn chairs. *What Gramma really meant was, 'Oh, to be seventy again!' Imagine that. Here am I, approaching forty and thinking I'm over* the hill, while Gramma's longing to be *seventy* again. When her husband and son were still alive. Still working a half-shift at the bakery. In relatively robust health. The economy was good. It was peacetime. Boy, here's to seventy!

2

'I couldn't make you crispy squares, dear.'

Gwyn expressed genuine sadness saying so. Not because her granddaughter wouldn't have them to eat. Because she couldn't make them.

'My hands have gotten so bad.'

Roxanne could see her gramma wasn't exaggerating. Her hands still looked like hands, but they were twisted with arthritis, her knuckles greatly enlarged.

'That's fine, Gramma. I don't mind. Besides, I can make them for myself. For us!'

'I can't eat them anymore, dear. But, thank you. I had Tina pick up a big box of crispies cereal, and the marshmallows.'

The housekeeper left after finishing Gwyn's hair. She came in three or four hours a day and did a bit of everything around the house: cleaning, cooking, helping Gwyn with bathing, and running errands. Whatever was helpful.

'Do you still hear from Jean, Gramma?'

They always talked about the same things, especially when she first arrived. Most always, at least. Occasionally, her gramma surprised her with a story or tidbit of information she'd never heard before.

'We talk every night at about eleven, before we go to bed. She's four years older than me, dear. Did you know that?'

'Yes, Gramma, you've told me before.'

Roxanne had spoken with Jean only once. A positively thundering voice, with an almost incomprehensible Scottish burr.

'After all these years, I still don't always understand what she says. My hearing is not that good anymore.'

'I'm not sure it's your hearing, Gramma.'

'What's that?!'

The timing and delivery were send-ups of the old music hall comedians. At Blackpool, or Brighton. *'Mind if I smoke? . . . .'* Short snappy roll on the snare drum. *'I don't care if you burst into flame!'* Thrummp, *tish* on the cymbal.

Her gramma smoked for more than fifty years, Roxanne thought in passing. Good thing she stopped, as she wouldn't be able to buy her brand now. Black Cat. With 'cork tips,' which meant a length of heavier paper — printed in flecked brown to resemble cork — was wrapped around one end to prevent tearing, or the paper sticking to your lip. A relic still visible on many brands, although most today wouldn't know the reason for its colouring.

'I said, *I don't think it's your hearing, Gramma.*'

Roxanne was always at pains to assure her gramma her decline was not as bad as it seemed; although it was, or worse.

'She has a thick accent, Gramma.'

'Oh, I've gotten used to that! We worked together at the bakery for twenty-three years, you know. She retired four years before me. We stayed in touch, but even more so in recent years, it seems.'

The only ones still surviving, Roxanne thought. Their friends, husbands, and children, all gone. Jean has two grandchildren, down in Seattle, and Gramma one. Me.

'Help me put my feet up, dear,' Gwyn sighed wearily. More than anything, she found her infirmities tiring.

'You never think of yourself as growing old or helpless. Inside, you're always just *you*.'

Roxanne felt a chill run up her spine, looking into her gramma's eyes. She'd seen that look before. Calm, meditative, penetrating. Extra lucid, somehow, as though her physical suffering and hardship resulted in transcendent moments from time to time.

The foot-stool, another museum piece, was a squat cylinder of transparent plastic inflated with air like a beach ball, standing on three short wooden legs. Plastic flowers were mounted on the base inside the stiff balloon. When she was little, Roxanne once asked her gramma how they got the flowers inside the bubble, like asking a model-maker how he got the ship inside the bottle.

'Can we look at pictures, Gramma?'

'We always look at pictures, dear.'

'I never tire of it.'

She didn't. Gwyn could tell from the tone of her voice that she was sincere.

'Okay, dear. You know where the books are.'

Roxanne went to the bookshelf in the front bedroom and came back with one of the albums. There were three altogether — two of Wales dating from 1910 to 1920, and one of Toronto between 1929 and 1932. Gwyn immigrated to Toronto in May of 1929 with her husband and nine-year-old son — on the promise of prosperity, on the allure of escaping the mines.

Although Gwyn's grandfather, a leader in the Welsh Independent Church, worked for the railroad in Swansea, the rest of the family were colliers. Her father was seriously injured in his thirties. He had a talent for mathematics, however, and was appointed to the prestigious position of weigher at their local pit. Gwyn's husband Albert was not a coal miner. He was a carpenter, from the west country. His family was Manx originally.

'There is Albert. And his brothers: Edgar, Geoff, and William,' Gwyn pointed out, after the exercise of moving to the sofa so they could sit together. Roxanne repositioned the bubble stool, and gently lifted her gramma's swollen legs back on top of it.

Roxanne knew their names and stories by heart.

'They all had English first names, Gramma.'

'Yes, dear. In the south country, when factories were opening and the railway was expanding, people thought their children might have a better chance of getting work if they had English names. We all still had Welsh family names; and you'd rarely mistake a Welshman, just like you'd rarely mistake a Scot.'

Gwyn's face tensed with emotion.

'Don't they look handsome, dear? Edgar was killed in the Great War. His widow, Enid, refused to accept the pension. Blood money, she called it. We were all Welsh-speaking then,' she said. 'When your father came to Canada as a boy, he had to learn his English. He could speak some, of course, but not properly. He decided that he was living in Canada now, and he would never speak Welsh again, which he never did.'

'Except when Great Uncle Geoff offered him the crown!'

'Oh, you remember that? Of course, you do. Geoff came to Canada once, in 1933, to see one of his musical friends in Toronto. We had a house out on the Danforth. Your grampa had to take in washing, you know, dear? There was no carpentry work for him. It was very hard. He learned he had something of a temper, then.'

So much sorrow and regret lies beneath so much of what she says, Roxanne thought. That was one reason she encouraged her to tell the stories. She knew it helped to reconcile those old sorrows, when she could tell her granddaughter something and see it was *not* a calamity, and that she was not scornful or disapproving.

'Those were hard times, Gramma. Grampa had no temper after you came out here to Vancouver during the second war.'

'Heavens, no. There was carpentry work for him here. He felt himself again.'

'What about the story in Toronto, when Geoff came to visit?'

'Goodness, yes! Geoff put the crown on top of a door and said, "Danny, I would like you to speak Welsh for me." If he'd tell him where the coin was, it was his.'

Gwyn smiled, and patted her eyes with a tissue. Six years earlier, at sixty-four, Danny had died suddenly.

She loved him above all else.

'He was a clever boy. He said, *"uwch ben y drws!"* — above the door! — and tapped the kickplate with his toe. Down came the coin, right into his palm, and away he went! That was the very last he ever spoke in Welsh, that I ever heard.'

'Did you know Great Uncle Geoff well, Gramma?'

'When we were younger, at home, I did. His brother Albert was courting me, of course. There weren't many men about during the war, you know, so I felt very lucky to have Albert's attention. Geoff was a couple of years too young to serve, so I often saw him then. He was always singing. Lovely songs. Beautiful words. A handsome boy, too. An angel.'

'They say he was a divine, Gramma.'

'He was, Roxanne, but not in the way they say. That playwright, especially, did not understand the truth.'

'It's good he'd be remembered in that way, though, isn't it? My girlfriend, Lindsay, performed in that play once. Gracious! What a long time ago! Almost twenty years.'

'The play was written about things that were *private*, things the writer did not understand. Bring me the picture of your father please, dear.'

Gwyn had an exceptional hand-tinted photo of her son, taken shortly after the war, on the mantelpiece. He was ruggedly handsome.

'Take off the back panel, please.'

Roxanne removed the back of the frame to find there were two other pictures behind.

'That one is your father's wedding picture.'

Roxanne was surprised. She'd never seen it before. Her mother passed away when she was an infant.

A flush came over Gwyn. Roxanne could see there was something about this photo that troubled her, something she feared Roxanne might find upsetting. Something that offended the deep propriety of her upbringing, her invincible honesty, her simple convictions.

'Your mother's dress is blue.'

Roxanne, puzzled for a moment, missed the meaning of her gramma's comment. A misguided fashion statement she could cope with.

'It's *blue*, sweetheart.'

Then Roxanne understood. She gave her gramma a big hug.

'Your father *loved* her. It didn't matter to him.'

'It doesn't matter to *me*, Gramma. I promise. It's nothing to me whether or not she was married before. It makes no difference to anything.'

'It only lasted a few weeks. One of her brother's buddies, a proper twit, and heavy-handed, too. Or, so I was told. They never had a home together.'

'It's okay, Gramma,' Roxanne repeated, traces of tears in her eyes. 'But, if it has troubled you, I'm very glad you could tell me now.'

'Your father loved her, Roxanne.'

Roxanne held her gramma tightly, relieved that this was all the crisis contained, saddened it had caused this grief. Needlessly.

'What's this other one?'

'That's the one I wanted to show you.'

It was a woman's face. She was attractive by today's standards. Roxanne wondered if she would have been thought beautiful in 1916, the date written in pencil on the back of the picture.

'This is Sarah. Geoff's wife.'

'I didn't know he was ever married, Gramma!'

Two revelations in as many minutes. She would not have thought, after so many visits, so many conversations, that there could be *any* yet forthcoming.

'She passed away in 1920. Influenza. There was an epidemic, dear, after the war. Geoff was deeply grief-stricken. He never talked about her again, except to Albert and me.'

Gwyn turned and looked into Roxanne's eyes. Roxanne could see there were other confidences to come.

'We spent time together during the war,' she continued, 'a private time, together, the four of us. That's when Geoff heard his music. He saw the angels, sweetheart, but he didn't first hear his music from them.'

Roxanne replaced the photos in the back of the frame.

'I'm tired now.'

She helped her gramma move her legs around to lie on the sofa for a nap. Gwyn was wearing the slippers Roxanne had given her for Christmas. A comic impulse. They were furry bear's feet, with big furry claws.

'You know, once I woke from a nap, sleepy-brained and without my glasses. I just about hit the roof when I saw those claws down there!' Gwyn laughed fondly.

3

Roxanne cooked dinner. Tina had left the kitchen spotless — as she always did — and had put out some chicken to defrost.

'What was it you wanted to tell me about Sarah, Great Uncle Geoff's wife?' Roxanne asked as they ate, sitting at the wooden dining table in the kitchen.

'Did I say there was something I wanted to tell you?'

'No, you didn't say, exactly, but I thought there might be. I sensed you'd like someone besides yourself to know the truth.'

'There is no *truth* to be known,' Gwyn stressed, 'only the thinking of your people. I *would* like you to know about your people.'

'I want to know! Especially the language. Working in the drug-store all day, I wouldn't have many opportunities to practise it, though.'

'You've done well in your profession, and I'm very proud of you, Roxanne. Your father was, too.'

Roxanne had wanted to be a musician when she was younger. She'd enrolled in the Faculty of Music at the University of Toronto in 1971; but, after completing two years, she decided there'd be no valid career for her as a full-time performer. So, she switched to pharmacy.

The music program had been enriching for her, at least, and she'd made a number of close friends — including the young actress who performed in the drama about her great uncle. They met after a Trinity College recital Roxanne and her friends performed at the time: they'd got chatting when it came out Roxanne was related to Geoff Douglas.

When they finished eating, Roxanne washed the dishes and helped her gramma to her chair in the living room.

'I'm still curious about Sarah, Gramma.'

'I believe she was one of the *Tylwyth Teg*.'

'The *fair-folk*? — do you really think so?'

'I do. When Geoff's family first came to Wales, they lived in Pembrokeshire. That's where Geoff came home with Sarah.'

'What do you mean, *came home*, Gramma?'

'When Geoff introduced her to his father and mother, she had no pedigree, so it was assumed she must be *Tylwyth Teg*, being so fair. That's what the expression means in Welsh, *fair-folk*, as you said a moment ago. Regardless, in the old country, new wives would usually present a history of their lineage, if they could.'

'Why, or when, could they not?'

'If they had no worldly ancestors or kin. Geoff told me his story of their meeting after Sarah passed away. One day, he went wandering away in the woods, hearing a song on the wind — a *luminous* song, he said. He found its singers; but, as soon as he saw them, they promptly disappeared.

'Then he noticed an old man behind him, a cheery old man with sparkling blue eyes. Geoff followed the man, hoping he might lead him home; instead, the man told him to remain absolutely quiet, and to follow him. They walked through the forest, until they arrived at a *menhir*.'

'What is that, Gramma?'

There was an awkward formality in Gwyn's voice, as though she meant to impress upon Roxanne that she was telling her something important; while also wishing to be relaxed, even casual, about it.

'A *menhir* is one of the long stones. The man tapped the stone with his stick. It opened, revealing a bluish light and a pathway below the ground. The old man told Geoff to come with him, down the path, on the promise that no harm would come to him. He did. Before long, they entered a beautiful fertile country, with fields, rivers, and mountains — and a palace. The palace was full of music — singing birds, and other songs — although Geoff could not talk, and could not see anyone, apart from the old man.'

'Is this where Geoff heard the voices on high, Gramma?'

'He heard the songs of his people there, but another more important time was yet to come.'

Gwyn rested momently, asking Roxanne to help her adjust the pillows supporting her lower back.

'A woman appeared with three young maidens. Geoff tried to speak to them, but could not — until one of the maidens kissed him, at which he found he could speak freely. He was charming, too. He made the maidens laugh.

'He stayed with them for one year, although he didn't think it was any more than a day. There came a time, however, when he wanted to see his family and friends, so he asked the old man if he could go home again. The old man asked him to stay a little longer, which he did. It turned out the maiden who had kissed him did not want him to go.'

'The maiden was Sarah?'

'That is correct, dear. He promised he would come back to her, and she believed him. She sent him on his way home, loaded with gifts.

'Back in his own village, his parents and brothers welcomed him warmly, marvelling that he could be away so long and return alive. But, none of his old friends recognized him, and he grew unhappy. Before long, he told his family he was returning to the *fair-folk*, as he had promised. He assured them he would be back soon.

'Sarah was very happy to see Geoff return to the palace. They both wanted to be married immediately. *Tylwyth Teg* don't like a lot of fuss about things, so they enjoyed a quiet ceremony. Afterward, Sarah wanted to return with Geoff to the upper world. Not only was she allowed to go, but the newlyweds were given two snow-white ponies as a blessing.

'They bought a cottage in Geoff's village with the wealth of the *Tylwyth Teg* that Sarah brought with her. They had sufficient left over to allow Geoff to study his music without having to take up a trade, or leave Pembrokeshire for the mines, to get along. Sarah was very beautiful. Everyone adored her.'

Gwyn looked over at Roxanne. Her face was bright. She had truly loved Sarah.

'Most of the villagers enjoyed the idea she might be *Tylwyth Teg* — although, knowing something of their nature and customs, they knew they had to be careful also. For example, a woman of the *fair-folk* could not be touched with iron, or tapped thrice on the shoulder, or she would disappear.'

Roxanne enjoyed hearing the story, as she might a bedtime tale, but she was puzzled, too. She didn't think her gramma was being absurd or silly. She was trying to *tell* her something: about Geoff and Sarah, of course — but, more than that, about her 'people.' It would take time to understand.

The phone rang. It was Jean. Roxanne saw her gramma turn down her hearing aid, which she thought curious, until she remembered the booming Scottish voice! Roxanne could clearly hear what Jean was saying, sitting more than arm's length away from the receiver at her gramma's ear.

They talked for about twenty minutes. How did they come up with so much to say every day? Of course, Roxanne knew that wasn't the point. It was the only contact either of them had with a friend, apart from househelpers and grandchildren.

'When was the last time you saw Jean, Gramma?' Roxanne asked when they were finished talking.

It was late. Time for bed.

'Not for . . . Oh, my gosh, fifteen years.'

'How far away does she live?'

'Not too far. Over near Arbutus, at 16th or so.'

'What?! Your friend is only twenty minutes' drive from here, and you haven't seen her for fifteen years?'

'There's been no one to take me, dear.'

That was true.

'Well, there's me, and I would have a long time ago, except I wasn't aware.'

4

The next morning Roxanne thought she should get out of the house. She had a habit of staying in when she visited, hanging at her grandmother's side the whole time. She'd discovered that even a cherished granddaughter could wear out her welcome.

It was hard for Roxanne to think of something she might like to do, however. Vancouver did not lack for entertainment; but, while she lived alone, she felt lonely walking around town on her own. She had no friends here, really.

Then, while brushing her teeth, she had an idea.

'Where to, Ma'am?' the cab driver asked. A Vancouver cab. A yellow Chevrolet, with shiny trim and chrome wheels. Funny how taxis in a given city assume a distinctive character, she thought.

Taxis in Vancouver all had these chrome wheels. Maybe the city required it! She imagined the little check boxes on the licence form: Commercial chauffeur's permit [*tick*], Photo identification [*tick*], Vehicle safety certificate [*tick*], Chrome wheels [*tick*].

'U.B.C.,' Roxanne said.

'Whereabouts?' the cabbie asked.

Usually she'd be going to the Japanese Garden.

'Wreck Beach,' she said, looking him square in the eye in the rear-view mirror.

'Sure thing,' he said with a smile, 'nice day to get a tan.'

Wreck Beach was exclusively for nude sunbathing. Roxanne wasn't clear if, strictly speaking, the City allowed it; but, it must tacitly ignore it as long as there was no trouble. It had been going strong for several years, so Roxanne assumed there had been no trouble.

For her part, she wanted to do something a trifle drastic and off-the-wall, something that might be fun. She needed to distract herself from her gramma's condition for a few hours.

She climbed down the long path, cut as broad stairs down the steep cliffside. This will be exhausting to climb back up! she thought. She did not have a towel or swimsuit along. She'd been obtuse about her needs for the outing, being so concerned about her gramma.

There were crowds of bathers there, almost all naked. Not always *completely* naked; but, in general, the women were at least topless and the men at least bottomless.

Roxanne kept her shirt on as she walked along, making as though she were looking for a place to sit. In fact, she was taking in the scene, trying to understand the etiquette and manners of the society.

Reaching the far end of the beach, she no longer felt reluctant to pull off her top. After all, *she* was clearly the odd one out! But she rolled her eyes and laughed when she realized she didn't have any sunscreen along either. She'd be toasted red in a second, lying naked in the bright inferno that afternoon.

'Caroline! Is that you?' She spotted someone she knew from Toronto, sitting on a towel, topless in blue jeans, and drinking beer.

'Roxanne! Great to see you. I didn't know you'd be out here in Lotusland!'

'Can I borrow a palmful of sunblock?'

'Of course. Help yourself.'

Roxanne pulled off her shirt and liberally covered herself with tanning oil. A woman happened by — wearing only a change belt and carrying a party cooler — to offer her a beer.

'Two bucks,' she said, and Roxanne asked for one.

'Beer probably isn't the best stuff to drink when it's this hot,' Roxanne said.

'Are you driving?' Caroline asked.

'No.'

'Drink up and enjoy!'

Roxanne felt Providence had smiled upon her, causing Caroline to be the person she bumped into on her excursion. She had been her pharmacist before becoming her friend. Caroline didn't have many friends back home. She was a true intellectual, a philosopher.

Roxanne enjoyed her thoughts and dialogue greatly, but most people didn't have time for it, and Caroline didn't have time for many of them. She had a couple of regular guys she'd see for a dirty weekend every now and then, but otherwise she kept to herself. She was living off a legacy, the proceeds of her mother's estate.

'I'm staying with my gramma,' Roxanne said, thoroughly enjoying the hot sunshine.

'Uh oh . . . Causing you a flood of grief and anxiety, in equal measure to the love you have for her, no doubt? She's quite elderly, isn't she?'

'Ninety-four yesterday.'

'You haven't got to believing in an afterlife, to ensure she will carry on, have you?'

'I hadn't really thought about that.'

'That's good. But, should the thought ever surface, set fire to it immediately.'

Roxanne laughed. Then she asked, 'Do you know about the Celtic resurrection myths?'

'She's Welsh, isn't she?'

'Yes.'

'Was she brought up in the country?'

'In the southwest.'

'It's quite an interesting construct, actually. For the Welsh seers, it was a matter of the evolution of souls, rather than death and rebirth in the usual sense. There were three "circles" through which a soul must pass. The first was *Cylch y Ceugant*.'

'You can remember the names?!' Roxanne said, interrupting.

'The encylopaedia,' Caroline sighed, pointing to her skull, 'is the sorrow of my life, but I try to make the best of it.'

She took a mouthful of beer, finishing her tin.

'The second circle was called *Cylch Abred*, the last was *Cylch y Gwynfyd*. Each of these names refers to spiritual training one undertakes in life. Each circle has to be brought to perfection. If you don't perfect a circle during a given existence, you arrive back there for the next. On the other hand, if you reach the perfection of a circle — circle two, for example — then you go to circle three next time.'

'What do the circles mean?' Roxanne asked.

'The first is unformed essence, like the nature spirits. Trees and whatnot. The second's roughly where we are now, meaning having a knowledge of good and evil. The third is a state of blessedness — although, unlike the Buddhists, say, you retained your individuality. All of your wishes and desires are in harmony, and you know God.'

While Roxanne was listening, she was absently watching a well-tanned man and woman, both strikingly handsome and muscular, playing with a frisbee. She got thinking about Geoff and Sarah.

'Gramma was telling me about my great uncle,' she said. 'What she said made me sad in two ways. Firstly, he met a woman who adored him; and secondly, she died of flu only a few years later. Nature can be so brutal.'

'But you would still take a few years with someone who adored you, and to hell with the suffering after they were gone, right?' Caroline looked away, and her voice softened. 'Me too.'

Roxanne's face fell. She looked at her friend with regret.

'I'm sorry, Caroline.'

'That's okay, never mind. I talked myself right into it. What else did your gramma say?'

'It wasn't *what* she said. It was *how* she said it. She had an odd way of telling me the story. There were surreal — or magical — parts. I'm not sure what to make of it.'

'Somewhere in her heart she knows her time is coming soon. When the time is near, *y gwragedd* (or womankind), start encoding their stories. It's a way of expanding beyond themselves. Taking what is personal and individual, and transforming it into something more general, about their people and their society.'

'It seems odd today, but I can see now that a hundred — or a thousand — years ago, in the old world, things were very different. That will be largely repressed now, especially in the fast-paced hilarity of our cities.'

'That's true. Although the fairy faith did survive the emergence of Christianity. Or the other way around, really. Had they not managed to assimilate one another over time, there would've been no Christian church in Celtic countries. The folk belief would have been the survivor of any impasse between the two.'

'But what were you saying about womankind, when they get older?'

'They suddenly see *themselves* as less significant,' Caroline continued. 'After all, they won't be around much longer! Instead, they see what will endure of themselves in their culture as significant. It's a way of redeeming the experience of their lives — a part of which they have passed on directly by having children and grandchildren;

another part of which, they realize then, must be passed along as knowledge, as a moral interpretation of the heart and feelings of their people.'

'You're very erudite,' observed Roxanne. After a moment, she added, 'What happens when *I'm* ninety, if I have no heirs for either?'

'We'll play cards,' Caroline said with a grin, 'and talk.'

5

'How was *All My Children*, Gramma?' Roxanne said as she came in the door. Tina was gone, but Roxanne knew the two of them had dropped everything for *All My Children* earlier in the afternoon.

'That man's wife is going to discover that letter soon,' Gwyn said, sitting in her easy chair, 'then there'll be trouble!'

It was the same up north on Baffin Island, Roxanne remembered. If they were late, someone told her at the time, the bushplane pilots would always radio ahead to have *All My Children* recorded on a videotape player.

Roxanne had visited the lead-zinc mine on Strathcona Sound with her friend Lindsay, the actress, ten years before. She wasn't performing, of course. She just thought it would be fun, a unique opportunity, and took advantage of the group's discount fares.

Heather and Harry, she thought. Imagine Heather meeting a guy like that, right out of the blue! Still so happy, after ten years! No such luck for me. Maybe I'm looking too hard. Or, maybe I'm not looking hard enough! Together with some of Gramma's firm propriety — which I would have had from my mother as a youngster. I don't want to get involved with a man unless I think I would want to marry him, which can be very hard to know at first.

Maybe, she wondered, looking in the wrong ways altogether.

Roxanne had endured a number of unfortunate false starts.

'Shall I make some dinner, Gramma?'

Gwyn smiled, and Roxanne commenced cooking.

When she was serving, she asked her gramma if she mentioned the idea of a visit to her friend, Jean.

'I haven't yet, dear.'

'Do you not want to go?'

'Yes, I do, but . . .'

'Are you nervous, after all these years?'

Gwyn smiled sheepishly.

'That's very natural, Gramma. And, if you decide you'd rather not bring it up with her, I will understand.'

'I *want* to go, Roxanne.'

'Okay, Gramma. I won't rush you, of course; but, I'm only here for another two days, remember. Otherwise, you can leave it until my next visit.'

Gwyn's face clouded slightly. Roxanne knew what she was thinking. Jean may not be alive when she next comes to visit. *She* may not be alive. She will not be in her own house.

They hadn't talked about her gramma having to leave her home. The doctor had given Gwyn four months maximum to ready herself, and had engaged a social services person to find her a room in a suitable extended care home. Roxanne planned to look at the place in the morning.

Gwyn knew she had to go, but could not bring herself to talk about it. Roxanne did not know how to bring it up. A tightly packed, explosive cylinder of fears, anxieties, and despair. Like Great Uncle Geoff sitting on the back of the bomb that finally blew him to bits during the war, she didn't want to hit the pin for her gramma now if she didn't have to. She thought that once she was in her new room at the home — and saw for herself that there was good food, good company, and good care — her fears would subside.

Roxanne would see the next day if, indeed, the food, company, and care looked like it was going to be okay. If it did, she'd return in a month to help with moving, although most of the work would be done by the home. They had experienced people.

Roxanne wanted her gramma to have the dignity of visiting her friend while she was still in her own house. Jean was still in her own house — although she had a day-nurse, and probably didn't have long to live.

'I'll ask her tonight, sweetheart,' Gwyn promised. 'We could go the day after tomorrow, after . . . .'

She almost said it. Her eyes filled with tears. She took off her heavy glasses and reached for a tissue. She couldn't find the box. Tears were streaming down her face.

Roxanne quickly came over to her chair, snapping up some tissues on the fly and taking Gwyn in her arms, as well as she could with the old woman sitting in her chair.

She gently dried her eyes.

'This is how you held me when you came to say Danny had gone. "I've lost my daddy," you said. I didn't understand you at first. Then I couldn't imagine it was possible. I wished it could have been me instead. It should have been me. I'm so old.'

'It doesn't work like that, Gramma. There is no justice in that scheme of things. No healing for those left behind.'

'He was a good man.'

'I know he was, Gramma. We didn't always see eye-to-eye, but I loved him with all my heart.'

'Parents and children will never always see eye-to-eye. It was the same with your father and his dad, especially through the troubled times we had after first coming to Canada. No one came to this country expecting the depression to hit like it did. For us, that was only weeks after we first arrived.'

'We'll be okay, Gramma.'

'You're a sweet young girl, Roxanne.'

'I love you, Gramma.'

'I love you, too, dear.'

Roxanne sat with her gramma for a few more minutes, feeling the two of them to be acutely isolated there, like a two-woman dance band on the *Titanic*.

6

Roxanne was chatty over breakfast, browsing the morning paper as she talked and ate. Her appointed task that day had been acknowledged — and better accepted — at some level, but was still left unspoken.

'Look here, Gramma, someone wants to build an airplane, to pedal over to the Island.'

'To pedal?'

'This was one of the great achievements in the history of man, Gramma, but it hasn't seemed to penetrate the popular consciousness the way it deserved.'

'What was that, dear?'

'Human-powered flight. For centuries, mankind had been trying to get off the ground with sheer muscle power, but only succeeded about ten years ago. Just ten years ago! A couple of guys built an ultra-light plane, with a propeller that turned by pedal power. One of them flew across the English Channel. One of the great achievements of civilization!'

'It must have been a very athletic young person, to be able to pedal for three or four hours, or whatever it took,' Gwyn observed.

'*Very* athletic indeed!' Roxanne nodded, pleased her gramma had grasped the idea so clearly.

'Jean will be expecting us this afternoon at four o'clock.'

Roxanne was pleasantly surprised to hear her say that.

'Don't look so worried, Gramma, that's wonderful! It will be fine.'

'I haven't been out visiting like this for several years, Roxanne. I have to work up to it somewhat.'

'I know that. It'll be okay.'

'Before you go.'

'Yes, Gramma?'

'I would like to tell you something. A story. About the old country. About our home in the old country.'

Gwyn had that *look* in her eye. Roxanne certainly was not going to decline.

'Let's sit in the living room, Gramma.'

Once seated, Gwyn began her story. It was clear to Roxanne she'd been thinking about it for some time, and knew exactly what she was going to say. Probably she'd rehearsed it in her mind.

'Albert was left some land in Dyved, and, in a gesture between brothers, he offered Geoff a partnership in it. Geoff said he had no desire to own more land — he and Sarah were comfortable with what they had from the *fair-folk* — but, in the spirit of friendship, he accepted, and we moved from Pembrokeshire to our new home.

'Albert and I were married there, shortly after we arrived. Geoff had told Albert I was the finest woman he could ever find, and that he should not delay. It was good land, with wild game and honey. There were two cottages at its corners. Geoff settled in one, Albert in the other. We were happy there.

'One day, when we were out walking, a thunderstorm came upon the four of us. We found shelter; but, as we did, a thick black fog came down over the land. When it lifted, the animals were gone. More than that, when we returned to the village we discovered all the people were gone. A long time passed — many months — and still, we were alone.

'Albert decided that we could not go on like that, so we left Dyved and travelled to England, to Hereford. There were some people there — though only women — who told us that a blackness was over the whole of Europe.

'Geoff and Albert opened a shop in the village market, for leather goods. Albert was very talented at it — especially the colouring of the hides — so, as long as there was leather available at their store, no other shop sold a single length. They became unpopular because of this. "Between me and God," Albert said, "I think we should leave, and go to another town." So, we did.'

Roxanne paid careful attention, deciding she would have to listen now and understand later.

'We travelled further down the Wye, still on the English side, and settled in another village where Geoff and Albert worked as gold-smiths. Geoff had a particular talent for this. He made buckles, especially, of great beauty. But, the same thing happened there with the other tradespeople, so we decided to go, before their rivals drove them away.

'At the next town, near Bristol, they became tailors, hopeful that the seamstresses of the village would not similarly conspire against them. Of course, they did. Albert and Geoff made such a fine suit of clothes that, if they had one ready, no other shop in town could sell what they had.

'We decided, then, to return to our home in Wales. We had some dogs, and made our way by catching small game. There were still no people to be seen in Dyved.

'One day, while we were out, the dogs strayed to a copse — but bolted in alarm when they got close. A shining white boar had chased them away. We followed the boar, and it led us to a great fortress.

'Geoff and I entered by the front door. Inside, there was a marble fountain surrounded by women of the ancient days, singing.'

'This is where Geoff heard the music?'

'Yes, dear. He went to the fountain, and sang with the exalted. They could see he loved music, and understood their song in his heart. The chorus swelled, growing ever louder, more complicated, and more beautiful.

'One of them told Geoff his sympathy demanded they teach him the song of the other circles — the songs of all the world — and he would have knowledge of the whole world.

'Albert and Sarah could hear the songs from outside, but as the sound came to a great crescendo, the fortress — with Geoff, the maidens, and me — vanished.

'Albert didn't know what to do. Many weeks passed with no sign of our returning. Albert decided he would take Sarah back to England, where they might earn some money to give to a seer to find us.

'On the way to Hereford, however, Albert and Sarah were camped, and Albert caught a pixie. He called to a second one that escaped, saying that if the spell over Dyved, and the fortress, were not lifted, he would hang the other he'd caught in the morning.'

'Is this *true*?' Roxanne blurted out. She knew it wasn't the right question to ask, but she was shocked at the idea.

'This is the spirit of your people, Roxanne.'

'Sorry to interrupt, Gramma.'

It did not sound to Roxanne quite like her gramma, anyway. But, her tone was warm and assured, and gave Roxanne no real cause for worry.

'At the first sun, Albert walked down the road, with the pixie tied up in a leather bag. A scholar came down the road the other way. "Good day to you, Sir," he said, "what are you doing, pray?" "You are the first man I have seen in this land in a year," Albert replied. "I am going to hang this pixie for imprisoning my wife, the husband of my friend, and my county." "That would surely be below your mettle, Sir. Here, I will give you a pound to let the creature go." "I will not," Albert said, and the man went on his way.

'A few minutes later a priest came down the road in a carriage. He also begged Albert to let the pixie go, and made an offer of money. "I will not," Albert replied. He offered him even more money, and horses. Again Albert said no.

'The priest asked Albert what price he would name. "The release of my brother, Geoff, and my wife Gwyn." "You shall have that," he said. "That is not all," Albert added. "What else?" the priest said. "The lifting of the spell over Dyved," Albert said. "You shall have that," the priest replied. "Now, free the pixie." "I will not," Albert replied, "I want to know who this pixie is." "She is the Empress of the Island over the mist bridge," the priest said, "otherwise I would not ransom her."

'Then Albert asked, "How did she come here?" "You should rather ask why she left," the priest said, revealing herself as a priestess of the mist. "Now release us." "I will not," Albert said. "What else do you wish?" the priestess demanded. "You must promise that no revenge will be taken upon us." "You are wise to ask that," the priestess said, "else we would have burned you to ash." "I will release her now," Albert said, seeing Geoff and me approaching over the croft.

'The Empress spoke to us, saying that they had returned to the land of men after all the centuries, knowing a grave plight had descended over Europe, as there never had been before. She said they had enchanted the land of Dyved to hide it — so no one would know it was there, and it might escape.

'Albert replied, saying that men had to fulfill their destiny. He asked her why they had left in the first place, if they cared for the land, and for men, so much. "We did not leave," she said. "We retired away, because we were forgotten."

'They sang for us then — a song to tell us they were returning to the Apple-Land.'

'Is that Avalon, Gramma?'

Gwyn was silent, her eyes closed.

'Gramma?' Roxanne moved closer.

Having finished her story, Gwyn had fallen fast asleep with the exhaustion of telling it. Roxanne could hear her breathing softly.

'That was a wonderful story,' she whispered.

7

Roxanne returned from the nursing home to find that Tina had helped Gwyn to get dressed, before she left for home. Gwyn was sitting in her chair, looking like she was prepared to greet the Queen of England.

'What a beautiful dress, Gramma!'

It was a smart blue woollen jacket and skirt, cut in crisp formal lines. Something in which you'd stand out at a wedding, though perhaps be a little overdressed for church on just any old Sunday. Under the jacket she was wearing a sheer white blouse with lace trim, along with a string of white pearls.

'You will have to help me with my shoes, dear.'

'Of course I will. Gramma, I don't have anything along to get dressed up like you are.'

'Am I dressed up?' Gwyn said coyly. 'I just wanted to wear something nice.'

'You are *stunning*, never mind!'

'Thank you for taking me, Roxanne.'

'I couldn't be happier.'

'I think the best you can do at my age,' Gwyn said, 'is to be peaceful inside.'

'Yes, Gramma.'

'Does that sound commonplace to you, dear?'

'I guess it does. A little.'

'Some ideas are simple and plain over all the years and, Roxanne, I know only this: Whether you live long or short, rich or poor, healthy or sick — in the end you are alone with yourself inside. So, you had better be comfortable with yourself. Had better *see* yourself. And enjoy yourself.'

'Isn't that a bit selfish?'

'Not at all. It only means that you have to discover what those things *are* that you love, and emphasize them in your life. It doesn't mean that they don't include giving, and sharing — and there will be joys *and* sorrows. *To every thing there is a season*, dear.'

'You sound like Great Uncle Geoff's friend, Erin Powell, in the play, Gramma!'

'That is nice of you to say, sweetheart. I never met her, but Geoff wrote to me that she — the real person, I mean, not the one in the story — was wise, and had a kind heart.'

'I don't think very many people are kind, Gramma.'

'People can become twisted, dear, if their understanding of others has been through cruelty, or violence. They become lost to themselves, and may feel a gruesome satisfaction about their lives, but never peace. There was a man who cheated Albert in business when we first arrived here. For twenty-seven years, whenever he heard his name, Albert would say, "Is he not dead yet?" How satisfying could that be? It is so easy to be a generous spirit to people instead.'

'So, you find redemption in a peaceful heart?'

'If you truly *have* a peaceful heart, thoughts of redemption will rarely come to mind.'

Roxanne paused to think.

'It's hard to avoid trouble in your life.'

'Sweetheart, what I tell you doesn't mean shutting things down upstairs. It means doing what you can to leave things in the best state you can. It means sharing what you can, saying goodbye where you can, and finding peace and forgiveness.'

'You don't need anyone's forgiveness, Gramma!'

'Of course I do, dear. Everyone has done wrong in their time — I have hurt people's feelings, and let people down. I know I have. But the trouble is, you don't always do something about it at the time. Then, when you get to my age, there's nothing you *can* do, because they're gone.'

'You mustn't worry yourself.'

'I'm not worrying, sweetheart. On the contrary, I'm trying to tell you how grateful I feel, having had time to think about things, set some things straight, and do what I can. Your Great Uncle Geoff did not have that chance. *Poof!* He was gone. I know he tried to be giving, and to help people, in his last years.'

'That's true,' Roxanne said.

'Albert, Geoff, and especially your father would have wanted you to know the love they had for their country. The old country. What it meant to them.'

'You have given me that, Gramma. I will try to understand even better, as well as I possibly can. But, Gramma, we're talking like this is your last day! You've got a while in you yet!'

'That may be, dear. I can't be sure. I do know it will not be the same when I have left this house.'

'Oh, Gramma, don't be silly.'

Roxanne wanted to be reassuring, but she didn't think it was silly at all. This was the essence of her gramma's story. Knowing where you belong, and are valued, and useful.

The story's ending was important, too. The Goddess describing her withdrawal from the world, forgotten. For her gramma, that was about dying, Roxanne thought. Passing away.

'Gramma.'

'Yes, dear.'

'Love means a lot, you know. You need all of the things you said, but they are no good without love. Love unlocks their magic. This is what you have given me, above all else. Not just now, but through my entire life. This part of you will be with me. Always.'

'Thank you, Roxanne.'

'We'd better get going, Gramma. Jean's waiting to see you!'

A Sweet Comedy *was made*
possible by the generous assistance
of the following individuals in
the arts and theatre communities

LORRETTA BAILEY

CECILIA DI BENEDETT

STEPHANIE GRAHAM

ERIN KEANEY

L.V. KELLY

ROD MAXWELL

KELLY STEPHENSON

RENNIE WILKINSON

TOM WOOD

and (especially)
JEAN STILWELL

Thou hast great allies;
Thy friends are exultations, agonies,
And love, and man's unconquerable mind.
— William Wordsworth